"Stay," _encir..._ _...ong_ _finger..._

There was surprise in his eyes now, and he didn't look particularly happy about saying it, but he also didn't let her go. "I bared my soul. Isn't that worth a drink *and* dinner?"

The touch felt so good. The warmth peeled back several layers of protection that hid her loneliness from the rest of the world. It had been so long since a man had touched her, casually or any other way. And nearly as long since she'd allowed herself to consider having dinner with a man.

She simply couldn't make herself pull free.

If she hadn't really wanted to stay, it would have been easy to walk away. And if she'd just walked away, everything would have been fine.

Dear Reader,

On a plane recently I was making small talk with the woman seated next to me. I was tired and mostly wanted to close my eyes, but I didn't want to be rude during the forty-five-minute flight from L.A. to Las Vegas and we ended up sharing information about our jobs. An avid reader, she was excited to meet a published author, which is flattering because I don't consider myself all that exciting. Then she posed a question no one has ever asked before. How do I name my characters and do I ever change the names?

The first part of my answer was easy. In a continuing series I keep a list of existing characters and try to make sure no two names start with the same letter. In my humble opinion it's less confusing when a reader is trying to keep everyone straight. For *Her McKnight in Shining Armor* I did change the heroine's name. Starting a book is never easy, but this one was more of a challenge than usual. Originally I called her Emma but was having trouble getting this character to talk and decided to change her name. She's a Texas girl and I wanted something very Lone Star State. The TV show *Dallas* is set in Texas and when I ticked off the characters, Sue Ellen struck a chord. A "voice" began to form. But she's not a Sue or Susie, so I settled on Ellie and the name felt right. I had her voice and Chapter One took off.

A hero is only as satisfying to the reader as the strong, sassy woman who wins him over. Ellie Hart sashayed into Blackwater Lake on her four-inch heels and rocked Alex McKnight's world. She was an incredibly fun character to create and I hope you enjoy reading her story as much as I did writing it.

Happy Reading!

Teresa Southwick

HER McKNIGHT IN
SHINING ARMOR

TERESA SOUTHWICK

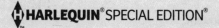
HARLEQUIN® SPECIAL EDITION®

Recycling programs
for this product may
not exist in your area.

ISBN-13: 978-0-373-65753-7

HER McKNIGHT IN SHINING ARMOR

Printed in U.S.A.

www.Harlequin.com

TERESA SOUTHWICK

lives with her husband in Las Vegas, the city that reinvents itself every day. An avid fan of romance novels, she is delighted to be living out her dream of writing for Harlequin.

To Mary Karlik, a Texas girl and real-life heroine. You're one of the strongest women I've ever met and I'm proud to call you my friend.

Chapter One

Alex McKnight needed a woman.

More specifically, he needed his architect, who just happened to be a very hot woman. The fact that he'd noticed was a problem because he didn't date coworkers, or any other ladies in Blackwater Lake, Montana, for that matter. He had a business to run in this town and couldn't afford to feed the rumor mill and tick off prospective clients with stuff from his personal life.

A bigger problem was that the very hot female architect was two hours late for work, and that didn't bode well for completing the Mercy Medical Clinic expansion on time. He had projects stacked up like planes waiting to land and if this one ran behind all the rest could crash and burn.

He looked at his watch and swore softly. It was going on noon and still no word from Miss Suellen Hart. Tomorrow the cement foundation was being poured, and last Friday, when he'd spoken with her, she'd promised to fly out of Dallas in plenty of time to be here for the event on Monday.

"They don't call. They don't write. So much for promises," he mumbled.

Maybe he was a tad critical, but in his opinion, he had an excellent reason. His wife, *ex*-wife, had promised to love, honor and all the rest of that baloney. But vows hadn't stopped her from running back into the arms of the man who'd fathered the baby she'd let Alex believe was his. She'd ripped out the foundation of his life, and if that wasn't cause to be bitter, he didn't know what was.

Alex walked the wood form set in the prepared ground that would hold the cement foundation of the clinic addition. He inspected every weight-bearing wall support to make sure they were in the right place. It would have been nice for the architect to be here with him to corroborate his judgment, although that was just a formality. He knew his job.

Just then he heard a car squeal into the temporary parking lot for the clinic. He turned and saw the little compact, a rental from the airport, skid to a stop by the construction trailer. The door opened, and out swung the best-looking pair of legs he'd seen east of California, and the rest of her was just as impressive. She was wearing a red skirt and snug matching jacket. The coordinating four-inch heels had come-and-get-me written all over them.

She leaned back inside, showing a pretty good view of her backside, then pulled out a purse the size of a Toyota. Much as he might like to avoid her forever, Alex knew he couldn't, so he moseyed over to meet her.

Miss Suellen Hart smiled as if being welcomed to a garden party. "So nice to see you again, Mr. McKnight."

He'd met her when she'd come to town for meetings on the project and accepted the fact that she was a looker, but it wasn't nice to see her again. She'd asked him to call her Ellie and at the time he'd thought it was cute. But not anymore. This woman pushed his buttons, none of the good ones.

"I thought you were going to call me Alex."

"I forgot." There was apology in her Texas bluebonnet-colored eyes. "Not surprisin' what with being late and all. I am so sorry, Alex. I'm normally punctual to a fault, although you have no reason to believe that. My plan was to fly in yesterday and get settled, but Mother Nature had other ideas. Y'all know how ladies have an inclination toward changin' their minds?"

"I do," he said dryly.

"Well, in Texas they say if y'all don't like the weather, just wait a minute. My flight from Dallas was canceled because of thunderstorms, and I was stuck at the airport. Cell service was sporadic to nonexistent, and I couldn't get a call through. I got here as quick as I could from that cute little Montana airport just a hop, skip and jump down the highway."

That cute little airport was close to a hundred miles from Blackwater Lake on a winding two-lane road. With mountains all around cell service was notorious for cutting in and out. "Stuff happens."

"Y'all must think I'm a flake."

Not the first word that came to his mind. Especially when she spoke in a breathless Southern drawl that was a little gravel, a little honey and all woman. "That wouldn't be fair."

"I promise that no one works harder than me. Y'all won't be disappointed." She took a breath. "I do apologize. Am I talkin' too much?"

"No." Damned if he couldn't listen to the Southern comfort in her voice all day.

"I must have had a bucket of coffee. Don't you worry. It'll wear off."

Studying her more closely, he could see that her skirt was wrinkled as if she'd slept in it, and fatigue had carved dark circles under those big, beautiful eyes. It was a look that made him want to take care of her, and that was a habit he thought he'd learned to break.

"You're here now." He almost added *better late than never.* He didn't, because she was pretty enough to be tempting, which made never a better alternative. "I'll show you the office."

"Okay. I'm anxious to get started." She smiled brightly. "I swear Mayor Goodson and the town council won't regret they picked me for the job."

"Your bid was the cheapest," he said. "No offense."

"None taken. I needed the work. It has to be said that I didn't expect y'all to be one of those contractors who believes the architect relationship is terminated on completion of the construction documents."

"What you're really saying is you're glad I don't think your presence on the job is both a nuisance and an unnecessary expense."

"Those words would never cross my lips."

And very fine lips they were, he thought, then ordered himself to focus. On work. "I believe an architect has a critical role to play during construction, and this addition to Mercy Medical Clinic isn't like an ordinary house."

She nodded. "If it were simply exam rooms there'd be very little challenge, but the outpatient surgery center needs more in the way of electrical and plumbing."

"One of the reasons the town council accepted your bid was the fact that you agreed to absorb the expense of being on site during the construction process."

"To keep a project on track and within budget inspections are advisable a minimum of three times a week. As remote as Blackwater Lake is, sticking around seemed like a good idea."

"You must have really wanted the job." He studied her closely and saw her smile slip for just a moment.

"It's an investment in the future. Everyone's got to start their own business somewhere."

"Yeah."

Except Alex was pretty sure this wasn't her start. He'd read her resume, and there was a yearlong gap between college and when she'd gone to work for Hart Industries, her family's company in Dallas. He wondered what had happened during that year. Nothing good if it was left blank. But she could have fudged the dates and she hadn't. One point to her.

And none of that was his problem, since he hadn't made the decision to hire her. He just had to do his best with that decision. "Come inside."

"I just have to get some things from the car if y'all want to go on ahead."

"Can I take something?" he asked.

"No, I'm used to this." She opened the trunk, and he saw a couple suitcases inside. She grabbed a briefcase and several tubes that probably contained blueprints.

"Is that everything?" When she nodded, he closed it up and said, "Follow me."

Alex was normally a "ladies first" kind of guy, but if he walked in front, he wouldn't have to look at the way that tight little skirt wrapped her world-class butt in silk. And just like that he got an image of tangled legs and twisted sheets with all that long shiny brown hair of hers spread out on a white pillow.

Whoa. Alex couldn't believe he'd just thought about sex with this woman. Then again, he reasoned, it had been a long time. This reaction wasn't personal, just a man's normal response to a pretty lady.

He opened the trailer door and let her precede him inside. "After you."

"If y'all don't mind I'll just get to work and make up for lost time." She looked around. "Is it all right if I use that desk?"

"Help yourself," he answered.

She walked across the room and put down her expensive leather briefcase and gigantic purse, and let the unwieldy tubes fall haphazardly on the flat surface. She pulled out her laptop and opened it, all business now. But, damn it, she'd just driven in from the airport after a crappy trip, and the silence after her Southern fried soliloquy felt all wrong.

"Would you like a cup of coffee?" He pointed to the corner, where a pot was set up on a small table.

"Oh, Lord, no thank you. I think my head would explode."

"I guess you're staying at Blackwater Lake Lodge?"

"Actually no. They couldn't confirm a reservation for the length of my stay."

"I'm surprised." He walked over and rested a hip on the corner of the desk, then leveled a friendly smile at her. He'd been told it could bring a woman to her knees, but that wasn't his intention. He needed this job to come in early and on budget—in other words, go smoothly. The best way to make that happen was for the two of them to get along.

"I was told that spring and summer bookings are really up this year."

"That might have something to do with the recent publicity generated by the hotel's new executive manager. Camille Halliday," he added.

Ellie's brows pulled together thoughtfully. "Why does that name sound familiar?"

"She's part of the Halliday Hospitality family and apparently something of a wild child in her youth."

She nodded thoughtfully. "Right around the time I was here before there was a lot of talk about the press hounding her and a picture in the paper of her kissing your brother."

"That's right."

She nodded. "I met with Dr. McKnight, and he couldn't have been sweeter to me. Dr. Stone, too. We had several conversations about their expectations and suggestions for the clinic expansion before I drew up the plans."

"By the way, he's engaged now."

"Who?"

"My brother, Ben. To Camille Halliday."

"That's really nice." She smiled, then turned her attention to the laptop. "Now, I brought my own copy of the building plans, but I see y'all have the blueprints tacked on the wall—"

"Do you have a place to stay?" The question was nothing more than curiosity, he told himself.

"I'm sorry?"

"You couldn't get a room at the lodge, so where are you going to live while you're here?"

"Actually, Dr. Stone helped me out with that."

Apparently Adam had succumbed to Blackwater Lake's philosophy of neighbors helping each other out. The family practice doc had relocated last summer and rented an upstairs apartment from Jill Beck, a local woman. "What did Adam do?"

"He suggested I rent his old place, since he and Jill are engaged and living together downstairs."

"And?"

"Jill agreed to a short-term lease, something she doesn't normally do. But I guess she made an exception for me."

"You and Jill must have hit it off."

"We did. She even invited me to the wedding, since it's going to be right there on their property by the lake where I'll be living." A smile lit up her face like the town square at Christmas. "C.J.'s actually the one who insisted I had to come to the ceremony, because he's wearing a tuxedo. That little guy of hers is just as cute as can be."

"The kid is something else."

"Anyway," she continued, "I was relieved to find something, and the silver lining is that it's more homey than a hotel."

"It has great views of the lake and mountains." Right now Alex had no complaints about his view. Ellie Hart sure did brighten up a drab, boxy, portable construction trailer.

"A definite plus. But now..." Her tone turned regretful. "Y'all have been so nice, but I need to make up for bein' late on my first day. It's not the way to make a good impression. Time for me to get to work."

She'd made an impression all right. Time would tell whether or not it was good. And as testy as he'd been about her tardiness, he couldn't believe he was going to say this. "Look, if you need time to settle and unpack, take it."

"That's really sweet, but..." She shook her head. "There's a lot to do, and the foundation's being poured tomorrow. I need to check the fittings for the bearing walls and go over the next phase of the project."

"I already did that. So, unless you want changes—but I can't see why—the plans are good," he said. "Really good."

"Thank you for sayin' so." She allowed herself a small smile. "But I don't want to leave anything to chance."

"I respect that." He waited for her to respond, but she focused on her computer.

Finally she looked up. "Was there something else?"

"Just one thing." He folded his arms over his chest. The guy who'd been told he could charm the bloomers off a man-hating spinster had been sucked in by *her* charm, because he couldn't believe he was going to say this, either. "You were a couple of hours late through no fault of your own. It's okay to cut yourself some slack."

"All due respect, that's not how I see it." She met his gaze. "I'm a woman in a traditionally male occupation."

"If you're worried about gender bias, don't be."

"Y'all are a man, and you can't really understand why I have to earn respect." She lifted one shoulder in a shrug. "It's my responsibility to plan, design and oversee the construction of the clinic to make sure it's functional, safe, economical and environmentally friendly. It has to meet the needs of the people who work there and everyone who uses it."

"In my opinion, you left nothing to chance."

Alex had studied in detail the final construction plans, and he was impressed with her attention to local and state building codes, zoning laws and fire regulations.

"It never hurts to check and double-check. If alterations need to be made, the sooner the better. Otherwise the project could go over time and over budget. And everyone will be checking and watching just a little closer because I'm a woman."

That was why he was checking her out, and it was no consolation that he hated himself for it. Obviously she wouldn't want to hear that. So, he tried to put himself in her shoes, which wasn't easy since they were four-inch heels.

"I see where you're coming from, Ellie, but I've been

in the building business for twenty years. Fetching, carrying and learning the trade while I was in high school. In college they actually let me use tools," he added, gratified when his self-deprecation earned a smile. "Eventually I started my own company in Southern California."

"I thought you lived here in Blackwater Lake," she said.

"I do. About two years ago I opened a branch of the business here."

"Why?" She seemed genuinely interested.

To answer her fully would require him to reveal details about his personal life, and that was something he wasn't prepared to do.

"This town is a diamond in the rough. Word is spreading outside of Montana that it will be the next Aspen or Vail. It has a lot to offer recreationally during the winter and summer. Clean air and water make it an ideal place for a vacation home or settling in for retirement. There's going to be a building boom, and I wanted in on that."

"So y'all are ambitious and career-oriented."

"Yes." Partly because he no longer had a family, and work kept him too busy to think about all he'd lost.

"Good. I feel the same way."

He nodded his approval. "Already we have something in common."

"I'm tickled y'all understand where I'm comin' from."

"I do. It's nice to know we're both on the same page." And there was one more thing. "How about a drink tonight after work at—"

She held up a hand. "I need to stop y'all right there."

Maybe if he explained. "It's a McKnight Construction custom to buy the architect a drink on the first day of a new job. For luck. Call me superstitious."

The corners of her mouth curved up, showing off dimples and the delicate shape of her lips. But the smile didn't make her eyes sparkle this time. "I'm goin' out on a limb here and say that y'all don't often work with a female architect."

"You'd be right. What gave me away?" he asked.

"Again—out on a limb, but I'm willin' to bet that means y'all don't usually flirt with your architect."

"You're wrong about the flirting. This is just me being friendly." Did that sound as smarmy to her as it did to him? He really didn't mean it that way. "It's sort of like pouring a solid foundation that sets the tone for a good working relationship."

"Yes. Until it's not."

"You're saying the male/female work dynamic complicates things."

"I am." Conviction and determination made the Southern drawl even thicker. "You have my word that our working relationship will be just fine during regular business hours and won't suffer at all for lack of alcoholic beverages afterward."

The thing was, in theory he agreed with her, but in reality he really did buy a drink for his architect on the first day of a new job. Considering his strong reaction to Suellen Hart, he should have been grateful that she'd turned him down flat.

"Whatever you want." He stood and started to walk away. "But for the record, Ellie? 'No first-day drink' means I *am* treating you differently."

"Understood. And, Alex?"

He turned. "Yes?"

"I need to put something out there."

"Okay."

"I'm not being rude, just honest." She took a deep breath. "Don't let the short skirt and Southern accent fool you. I'm not anyone's idea of a magnolia blossom. I don't

wilt or have the vapors. I'm smart and I can do this job as
well or better than any man. And that's what I intend to
do. One bad experience can set a career back, and that's
not going to happen to me."

Again. She didn't say it, but the word hung in the air
between them. Offhand he'd guess someone at work had
hit on her, it didn't go well and her professional reputation had suffered. Getting a good recommendation from
the firm after that would be next to impossible and could
account for the twelve-month gap in her work history.

"All right. Duly noted, Ellie."

"Okay. Good." She turned her attention back to the
computer and tuned him out.

Alex returned to his corner and realized his hot female
architect had finally arrived, but now his problem was
worse. He needed a woman more than ever, and he made
a mental note to take this itch away for a long weekend,
somewhere no one knew him.

There were a lot of good-looking bachelors in Blackwater Lake, and Alex McKnight was number one on
the list as far as Ellie was concerned. Her friendly-yet-
professional facade had been sorely tested during these
past two weeks, and she was looking forward to some fun.
This wedding was shaping up to be just the thing.

Jill Beck and Adam Stone's evening June ceremony
was about to start. It was being held on the front lawn
of their house, downstairs from the apartment Ellie was
renting from them. She was sitting next to Liz Carpenter,
the receptionist at Mercy Medical Clinic, who was pretty
much the only person in town she knew other than the
bride and groom.

"Is this seat taken?"

Ellie didn't need a visual to know that voice coming

from just over her right shoulder belonged to Alex Mc-Knight. For the past two weeks the deep tone had been messing with her mind from nine to five. The rest of the time memories of it unsettled her. She looked up at him, and her breath caught.

If she'd been prone to having the vapors, this was certainly a vapors-worthy moment. In his dark suit, gray dress shirt, silver-and-black-striped tie, he could stop the world. Hers at least, darn it all.

His short, dark hair was neatly combed. Intensely brown eyes were fringed by dark lashes that made her think of hot kisses under a black velvet sky full of stars. She'd seen him at the end of a long day, several hours after five-o'clock shadow had set in, but no scruff was there now. His lean cheeks and strong jaw looked freshly shaven. She had the most absurd desire to touch his face, see if the skin was as smooth as it looked.

"Ellie?"

He was waiting for an answer to his question.

"Hi, Alex." She forced herself to smile at him. "No, this seat is free."

"Not anymore." He sat beside her and his jacket sleeve brushed her bare arm. Any second she expected sparks to flash between them. He leaned close and said, "You didn't have far to go for this shindig."

"Just downstairs." His breath tickled Ellie's ear, and the spicy scent of his cologne had her willpower waving the white flag of surrender. After that first day he hadn't treated her any differently from the rest of the crew. In fact, one of the carpenters was a woman, which had made her feel foolish for her declaration of independence. "I really think they invited me so I wouldn't make trouble with the local law when the party gets noisy."

He laughed, and his gaze traveled over her from the

top of her head to the pink-painted toes peeking out of her silver high-heeled sandals. "You look beautiful tonight."

"Thanks. Y'all clean up pretty nice yourself." That was an understatement. Part of her wanted to call him on the compliment, but they weren't at work and she needed to lighten up. "So, are you a friend of the bride or groom?"

"Both. Adam and I got to be friends when we were on the committee for the clinic expansion. He and my brother were determined to add on and upgrade equipment to better service the medical needs of the community. He's a good guy. I know Jill because I keep my boat at her marina."

"I'm guessing it's not a rowboat."

"You'd be right. It doesn't fit on top of the car." He grinned. "I take her to the other side of the lake on weekends when I really want to get away from it all. No cell reception."

"So, you pitch a tent over there?" she asked.

"Nope. The boat has a cabin."

With a bed? she wanted to ask. Fortunately the words stayed safely in her head, and he couldn't hear the *crash bang* of her heart that followed the racy thought.

Just then the trio of musicians began to play a soft wedding march. Everyone turned to the aisle, which was covered by a white runner and ran between the two groups of folding chairs. Moments later the blonde flower girl and dark-haired ring bearer walked by, followed closely by matron of honor, Maggie Potter. Then Jill, wearing a strapless, cream-colored satin-and-lace gown, walked by holding the hand of her seven-year-old son, who was giving her away. She was a stunning redhead, and C.J. took after her. He looked especially cute in his tuxedo.

Ellie glanced at the groom, waiting under a rose-covered arbor with his brother and the minister. Adam's expression said he was equal parts dazzled and in love as his bride stopped in front of him.

"Who gives this woman to be married to this man?" the reverend asked.

"I do." C.J.'s voice was loud and clear. "Adam's gonna be my dad for real now."

Ellie's throat clogged with emotion and tears filled her eyes. What was it about weddings that made her so emotional? She hardly knew these people, but the setting was beautiful and romantic. And the three of them were officially beginning their journey as a family. She felt a tear slide down her cheek. Then another. She brushed them away, hoping no one would notice, but a second later Alex was holding out a folded white handkerchief.

He leaned close and said, "I always carry one for weddings."

She smiled when he pressed it into her hand and moments later was especially glad to have it. The vows and a spectacular kiss had her sniveling like a baby. Immediately after the ceremony, the wedding party disappeared with the photographer for pictures. Guests stood and milled around on the grass or headed to the decorated tent nearby, set up with tables for dinner.

"Thanks. I'll return this after it's washed." Ellie held up the handkerchief. "For the record, I'm glad you were packin'."

"I always cry at weddings."

"Right." She laughed. "I'm completely mortified. You must think I'm a big baby. But I just couldn't help myself. It was such a beautiful wedding."

"Don't apologize. It *was* beautiful and nice to know some people get a happy ending." His tone was either wistful or bitter, and it was hard to tell which.

Feeling the way she did about him made personal questions a slippery slope straight into the fires of hell, but she couldn't keep the words in her head this time. "Who broke your heart?"

"What makes you think someone did?" After they stood, he put his hand on her elbow to guide her over the uneven grass.

The touch of his warm fingers threatened to short-circuit her thoughts. "What you said about happy endings implies that you didn't get one."

"I didn't. Mine failed in a fairly spectacular way."

She looked up expectantly but he didn't say more. "Would you like to talk about it?"

"Not really." But a devilish gleam slid into those smoky eyes and burned the shadows away. "Although I could be persuaded to. If you have that drink with me."

She wanted to. Technically it wouldn't be abandoning her principles about getting involved with a man at work because they weren't *at* work. "Okay."

They walked into the tent, where a bar was set up just inside the entrance. Alex ordered white wine for her and a beer for himself, then guided her to an unoccupied white-cloth-covered table in a secluded corner. Small white lights and flower arrangements of roses, orchids and star lilies transformed the interior into something magical.

As the setting and wine worked their magic on her, Ellie began to relax. He pulled out a chair for her, and when they sat and faced each other their knees brushed.

"So, tell me about your spectacular failure," she said.

"I was married."

Past tense. She appreciated the straightforward honesty. It was information the jerk at her very first job had kept from her. Just to be sure, she asked, "'Was'?"

"Divorced." He took a long drink from his beer, and

there was something so masculine about the way his neck muscles moved as he swallowed.

"How did you meet her?"

"On the job."

Wasn't that always the way? It was why she was ultra cautious now. The only problem with not trusting was the intense loneliness. Touching Alex even a little made her miss having a man hold her, kiss her. Love her.

"Was this in college?"

"Nope. I was the boss and needed an executive assistant. She was qualified. And beautiful. It turned into more." Even the dim lighting couldn't hide the way his mouth pulled tight. "Then she told me she was pregnant."

"So you married her."

"And convinced her to move to Blackwater Lake because it's a great place to raise kids."

"She didn't like it here?"

"Partly. Mostly she didn't like me all that much."

"Idiot."

He smiled. "I appreciate that."

Ellie was aware that she wasn't a poster girl for great instincts where the opposite sex was concerned, but she'd seen how Alex handled the people who worked for him with amazing fairness. They'd move heaven and earth if he asked. You didn't get that kind of loyalty by being a jerk.

"So you weren't the one to end it," she said.

"No. As it turned out, instead of proposing marriage when she said she was pregnant, the question I should have asked was 'Who's the father?'"

The meaning of his words sank in. "Oh, no—she let you believe you—"

"Yeah. I enjoyed having a son while it lasted." There was raw bitterness in his voice now. "Dylan was almost a year old when she said she wanted his real father to raise him."

She could see the truth on his face. "Y'all loved that little boy."

"I sure did."

"I'm sorry, Alex—"

"Don't be."

"It's not pity," she protested. "I'm sorry for that child because his mother is a moron. Y'all are probably better off, except that you miss that baby."

"He's not a baby anymore. It's been two and a half years."

"I shouldn't have made you talk about it. Especially on such a happy occasion." She looked around and saw that the tables were filling up with people ready to celebrate another couple's love.

"I'm not sorry." He tapped his bottle against her glass. "Got you to have a drink with me."

"That's true." Got her to soften a little toward him, too. Maybe more than a little, and that wasn't necessarily a good thing. She finished off her wine and stood. Applause erupted when the bride and groom, hand in hand, walked in with the wedding party trailing behind them. "I need to go find a table."

"Stay." Alex reached out and loosely encircled her wrist in his strong fingers. There was surprise in his eyes now, and he didn't look particularly happy about saying it, but he also didn't let her go. "I bared my soul. Isn't that worth a drink *and* dinner?"

Again, the touch felt so good. The warmth peeled back several layers of protection that hid her loneliness from the rest of the world. It had been so long since a man had touched her, casually or any other way. And nearly as long since she'd allowed herself to consider having dinner with a man. She simply couldn't make herself pull free.

Sitting back down, she said, "That would be nice."

If she hadn't really wanted to stay, it would have been easy to walk away. But she couldn't walk away and just hoped everything would be fine.

Chapter Two

The reception was just as beautiful as the wedding had been. Adam and Jill had their first dance as husband and wife. His brother, who was the best man, had made a toast to the happy couple. Maggie Potter, the matron of honor, had wished them a lifetime of happiness, and her words were particularly poignant because her own happily-ever-after had been cut short when her husband was killed in Afghanistan.

Dinner was delicious and the red velvet cake cut without incident by the newlyweds, as in no icing had ended up where it shouldn't have been. Servers were distributing pieces to the seated guests, and Ellie had taken a bite because it would have been bad luck not to. This was an excellent time for her to slip away. She needed to go because of how badly she wanted to stay, and that was all Alex's fault.

She looked at him as he chewed the last bite of his cake. "It's been a lot of fun—"

"Don't say it," he warned.

"What?"

"That you're leaving."

"Maybe I was going to tell you that this is the best wedding I've ever been to."

"No." He shook his head.

"I could have been planning to say that I was late for plate-spinning practice."

The corners of his mouth curved up in a heart-stopping smile. "I have a feeling you're not the plate-spinning type. No, your tone clearly leaned toward preparing for a quick getaway."

"I had no idea y'all were so perceptive."

"Well, I am. Lesson number one in not judging a book by its cover."

"And just how did I do that?"

"You thought I was just another pretty face."

That made her smile, because she just couldn't help herself. "Now you're fishing for compliments, Mr. McKnight. Y'all are attempting to get me to list all the reasons I know you're an intelligent man."

His brown eyes sparkled with interest. "You think I'm smart?"

"I know so." No one would accuse her of exemplary judgment where men were concerned, but she'd worked with him long enough to know he was no dummy. "Y'all handle construction crews with a firm, fair hand. Your budget is running five percent under the estimate, and no one in Blackwater Lake has a single thing to say about your personal life." And she'd done her subtle, yet level best to pry information out of the crew, but more than one person said there was nothing to tell.

"Maybe I don't have a personal life."

"Now you're underestimating me." She laughed. "Of course a man like you has one. It's just not here in town."

"I'm impressed." The statement neither confirmed nor denied. "But what do you mean a man like me?"

The kind who slides his arm across the back of a lady's chair, she thought as he did just that. "A man who's funny. Handsome. And smart enough to engage me in conversation to distract me from my objective."

"Which is?"

Her goal had been to leave, but now it was changing, she realized. Right now she was concentrating very hard to not notice how close his fingers were to her shoulder. The cap sleeve of her lavender chiffon full-skirted dress didn't offer a lot of protection from the warmth of his hand. Tension coiled in her stomach, and her breath caught as she waited to feel his touch.

"I really need to go."

Just then the music started up again as the DJ announced there would be dancing until the wee hours. Couples drifted onto the temporary wooden floor in the center of the wedding tent.

"How about one dance, then I'll walk you home?" Alex held out his hand.

Ellie stared at him. Cinderella escaped from Prince Charming after one dance at the ball, then her magic spell fell apart when the coach turned back into a pumpkin. The thought should have strengthened her resolve to go now, but it didn't. She told herself giving in was the better part of valor.

"All right." She put her hand into his and he tugged her to her feet.

Alex settled his palm on her lower back as he guided her to the dance floor. Then he slid his arm around her waist and pulled her loosely against him. She put one hand on his shoulder as he folded her other hand in his and rested them on his chest. It was such an intimate gesture that all her female hormones squealed with excitement. They moved easily together in time to the music, as if it wasn't their first time.

"You're a good dancer." His breath stirred wisps of hair on her forehead.

"So are you."

Along with *handsome, funny* and *smart,* she added *graceful* to his positive adjectives list. It was an effort to keep her breathing normal when she was feeling incredibly breathless. She would bet her favorite pair of sexy stilettos that any woman he took to bed would, for the rest of her life, remember and compare the experience to every one that followed.

Good Lord, where did that thought come from? Duh. It was impossible to be in his arms and not notice the broad shoulders and muscular chest. He made her feel fragile and feminine. How could she not wonder what his bare skin would feel like against her own?

Good heavens, it was hot in here.

Mercifully the song ended before she embarrassed herself. Alex didn't let her go as the next one started, clearly intending to take the inch she'd given him and stretch it into a mile.

Ellie slid out of his arms. "I have to go."

"I can't talk you out of it?"

It would have been pathetically easy, but she forced herself to say no. "'Fraid not."

"Okay. I'll walk you."

"That's really not necessary. I don't have far to go. What could happen?"

"In Blackwater Lake? Most likely nothing. But McKnight men don't leave ladies to see themselves home."

"How chivalrous."

His shrug said it was no big deal, but she didn't agree. She also didn't trust. Once burned, twice shy.

"I'll just get my purse."

She walked back to the table, where several guests were drinking coffee and nibbling cake. She slid the short-looped handle of her silver beaded bag over her wrist and said good-night. Since the bride and groom were in a romantic world of their own on the dance floor, she decided not to disturb them. She lived upstairs from the couple and would have an opportunity to say her thank-you at a more convenient time.

Outside the June air was cool and the sky bright with a full moon that reflected a silver path on the lake. Could there be a more romantic setting? She could see the dock stretching into the water and boats tied up there.

"Which one is yours?" The words were out of her mouth before she realized the question had formed.

"It's in the slip at the end, where the water is deeper."

She didn't know anything about watercraft but it was impossible not to notice that it was the biggest one in the marina. Probably a bigger boat needed the deepest water.

"Looks like a beauty." She angled right toward the covered porch of the house where the stairs beside the newlyweds' front door led up to her apartment.

Alex put his hand on her arm. "Want to see her?"

"The boat?" Stupid question and it was nothing more than a stall. Ellie knew he wasn't talking about a woman.

"Yeah."

It wasn't only the warmth of his fingers that tempted her to say yes, but the fact that she was also curious. She'd never been on a boat before. Her father and brothers were into airplanes.

"I would like to see her," she agreed. "A quick tour, then I have to call it a night."

"Okay."

She liked the way he put his hand on her lower back. It was protective and gallant. In the moonlight with several glasses of wine humming through her, it was hard to remember why it was so important for him to be off-limits. She would tidy up her priorities in just a few minutes.

After the relative silence of moving through the grass, the dull sound of their footsteps on the wooden dock filled the quiet night. There was an almost imperceptible movement on the walkway, reminding her it was floating. They passed several rows of moored boats before he guided her down the last one and to the very end.

"This is the *Independence,*" he said proudly.

There was a narrow walk space around the slip that encompassed and protected the watercraft. In the middle was an enclosed space for whoever was driving the thing. Behind it in the back was a place for passengers to sit and probably sunbathe. If she had to guess about the material it was made of, she'd pick fiberglass.

He gracefully stepped on board, then reached over and settled his hands at her waist, easily lifting her from dock to deck while she held on to his shoulders.

"Thanks." Her voice was a smidge breathless, and it had nothing to do with the walk.

He didn't seem to notice, just took her hand and showed her around the deck. He pointed out where the captain sat behind the wheel and the cushions on the back where passengers could relax and sunbathe.

"I'll take you below," he said. "Let me go down the ladder first."

"You're the captain."

In seconds the deck seemed to swallow him up, then a light went on. "Okay."

She turned as he'd done then grabbed the handrails and put the toe of her high-heeled shoe on the slat. Nothing about her descent was as graceful as his had been. There was only one step to go when her four-inch-heel caught in the chiffon hem of her dress and she lost her balance. Strong arms caught her and set her on her feet. With his hands on her waist and hers on his chest, they were facing each other and she saw the exact moment when the humor in his eyes turned to hunger.

There was only a split second of hesitation before his lips lowered to hers. After a nanosecond of shock, she gave in to the amazing turn-on of feeling his mouth devour hers, the fantastic sensation of his body pressed against her. She couldn't get enough. He teased and taunted her with his tongue and tasted like beer and red velvet cake.

Backing her against the wall, Alex barely grazed his hips to hers and set off a firestorm of desire that swept through her. He dragged off his suit coat, then loosened his tie and yanked it over his head without untying it. Ellie tugged the dress shirt from the waistband of his pants, but before she could do another thing he turned her and unzipped her dress. She let it slide to her ankles. They were on his boat and she wasn't sure if she was light-headed from his drugging kisses or dizzy from the slight rocking.

She wasn't wearing a bra, and when Alex reached around and took her bare breasts in his hands, she could have been on a rocket ship to the moon. The way she felt right this minute left no doubt that she was participating in probably the best foreplay of her life.

Ellie turned and threaded her fingers in his hair when he took the peak of her breast in his mouth. She held him where he was, to keep him doing what he was doing. But when he stopped, she braced her hands on his hips and pulled him to her. "Alex, I want you—"

His gaze burned into hers. "I know how you feel—"

"Now. Please."

"Not here. The bedroom—"

"It's too far."

Grinning, he said, "That's where you're wrong."

He moved her a step to the side and into a room—cabin—that felt like wall-to-wall bed. He yanked down the coverlet then scooped her into his arms and settled her in the center of the firm mattress. Ellie kicked off her high-heeled shoes and slid out of her panties while he removed the rest of his clothes, pulled a square packet from his wallet then joined her on the bed.

She saw him tear open the condom and cover himself then could barely catch her breath as he nudged her legs apart and covered her body with his. Gently he entered her, and just like dancing, this didn't feel like the first time. She accepted him easily and found his rhythm. He moved inside her, building tension until she could hardly bear it. When he reached between their bodies and caressed the bundle of nerve endings at the juncture of her thighs, the instantaneous explosion of sensation stopped her world. Her breath came in ragged gasps.

Alex held her and whispered words she couldn't comprehend in her pleasure-drenched state. When she could think again, she wrapped her legs around his hips and urged him to his own release, using her body to tell him what she wanted to give. In a matter of seconds, he groaned and went still, holding her tightly as he found his own release.

Ellie had no idea how long they stayed wrapped in each other's arms before he rolled away and disappeared. A minute later he returned to the bed and pulled her against him.

With her head on his shoulder she said sleepily, "Y'all are pretty...awesome."

"Back at you, El." The words dripped with weariness and it felt as if he wasn't giving her a nickname as much as too tired to say her whole name.

She knew how he felt. She was too tired to keep her eyes open, so she didn't. Before falling asleep, her last thought was that she really should go to her own place.

Alex opened one eye when he heard a gasp beside him in the bed. It only took him a second to figure out that Ellie knew where she was, who she was with, what they'd done and that she was still naked. Dawn was just starting to peek through the window above the bed and her expression was easy to read.

He raised onto his elbow and looked down at her. "Hi."

"Good morning." She pulled the sheet up to her neck.

Her hair was spread out like brown silk on the pillow and looked sexier than hell. He badly wanted to run his fingers through it again. This probably wasn't the time to tell her that the whole sheet-to-her-neck thing was as much of a turn-on as seeing her stark naked. Her body was outlined and he could make out every one of the slender curves he'd very much enjoyed exploring the night before.

"What's wrong?" He knew something was bothering her by the way she chewed nervously on her bottom lip. He'd had a taste of it himself last night and wouldn't have minded another of that, either.

"I suppose we have to talk about this." Her expression said she'd rather walk barefoot on hot coals. "Like a bad cliché, I actually hate myself in the morning."

"We could pretend it never happened."

"Much as I'd like to slip quietly off y'all's boat, Hastings Hart taught me to face situations head-on and play fair."

A woman playing fair would be a refreshing change for him—if she'd actually learned the lesson from Hastings Hart.

"Your father?"

"Yes."

He nodded. "For what it's worth, I didn't bring you here with the intention of seducing you. It just—"

"—happened," she finished, studying him. "I believe you. And I didn't come with you to be seduced."

"So we're even."

"It was a mistake, Alex, and I take full responsibility."

He'd made his own mistake, but that wasn't what she meant. "What about we go fifty-fifty on the blame?"

"That's fair." She turned on her side, hand pressing against her chest to keep the sheet in place. "But here's the thing..."

This had to be the weirdest post-sex-talk-in-bed ever. "I'm all ears."

"If only that were true," she muttered. "We're working together. I make it a rule never to sleep with a coworker."

"I hate to break this to you but that ship has sailed." He looked around the cabin and added, "No pun intended."

"Thanks for pointing out the obvious," she said dryly. "I was here. But this really can't happen again."

"You sound pretty adamant about it." Although he agreed in theory, part of him wanted to take the words as a challenge.

"There's a good reason for that." She lowered her gaze and long thick lashes stood out against the smooth skin above her cheek. "In college I was at the top of my class and interned with one of the best architectural firms in Dallas. They hired me after graduation and I was on my way. Finally, I was going to prove to my father and brothers that I could take care of myself."

"What happened?" Something must have, or she wouldn't have been defensive the first day she'd arrived. And she seemed to have a rule against sleeping with co-workers. Some day he might regret participating in the rule breaking, but not right this minute.

"I got involved with one of the partners, but he neglected to tell me he was married."

"Sounds like a big company. No one else clued you in?"

"It should have been a red flag that he wanted to keep the relationship just between us. No one in the office knew. My bad that I believed his explanation about protecting me from employees who would resent my upward mobility and chalk it up to our relationship."

"How did you find out?"

"His wife caught him. Email. Cell phone." She gripped a handful of the sheet covering her breasts. "It doesn't matter. But she chose to out him in a very public way. She came to the office and confronted me."

"There was an ugly scene." It wasn't a question.

She nodded miserably. "No one believed I was that naive and didn't know he was married. They're a conservative firm, and questionable behavior in the workplace was against company policy but they did me a favor and let me resign instead of firing me."

Big of them, he thought angrily. So being fired wasn't on her résumé, but she also couldn't use her only work experience for a reference. "What did you do?"

"I left quietly and went to work for Hart Industries with my brother Lincoln. He runs the development branch of the company for my father."

"Not a bad gig."

"It was for me." She smiled sadly. "Harts have long memories and I'll never live it down, how I'm not so good at taking care of myself. I just want them to be proud, but now I've got to dig out of a really big hole."

"This is where I point out the obvious—the guy is a bastard." His tone was surprisingly even considering how angry he was.

"Y'all are preachin' to the choir. But that didn't change the fact that I had to lay low and let the dust settle. That was two years ago, and Mercy Medical Clinic here in Blackwater Lake is my second chance. There's no way I'm going to mess it up. It's time to reinvent myself, and mistakes aren't an option."

"I agree with you."

"You do?" She sounded surprised, as if expecting some pushback.

"I'm a businessman, and most of my business is here in town. It's small and getting involved with anyone is a very bad idea. When a relationship ends, and it always does, there can be hard feelings, word spreads, people take sides." He shrugged. "None of the above is good for McKnight Construction."

"So you really do have a personal life," she said, her voice full of *I knew it.*

"Yes," he agreed. "I just take it somewhere else for a long weekend."

"I see." She met his gaze. "So, we're in agreement."

"We are. I respect the fact that you don't play fast and loose, but that's the only way I want to play. Nothing gets in the way of my work, and it's important that the expansion is completed on time and within budget. I have projects and a reputation to maintain. Delay isn't an option for me," he said, echoing her words.

"I'm glad to hear that." She glanced up at the window. "So what do y'all think are the chances we can keep last night a secret what with the whole town at the wedding?"

"You live on the property and have a very good reason for your car being there. And I've been known to spend the night on my boat." He saw her look and grinned. "To sleep."

"Uh-huh."

He ignored that. "What I'm saying is that no one will think twice about my car still being here."

"I'm tickled to hear that."

"You just need to get back to your place before the newlyweds and their curious little guy are up and around. They're leaving on the honeymoon later today, but if they spot you in yesterday's dress, questions will be asked."

"So I better get going." She started to get up, then looked at him.

"I guess you want privacy." A little late for that, he thought. He'd seen, touched and kissed a lot of that soft skin and would remember last night for as long as he lived. "I'll leave you alone."

He didn't care if she peeked at him and threw back the sheet, taking his time to gather up his clothes before leaving the cabin. Just outside he saw her dress and picked it up. After rubbing the sensuous silk between his fingers, he put it on the bed. "You'll need this."

Something else she wouldn't want to hear was that he liked her dress a lot, but much preferred her without a stitch of clothing. Maybe just the high heels.

The thought made him smile until another, more sobering one took its place. There was one more thing he had to talk to her about.

By the time he had his pants on, Ellie emerged all dressed. She headed for the ladder that would take her topside. "See you tomorrow at work."

"Just a second."

With a hand on one of the rungs, she glanced at him. "What?"

"Is there any chance you're on the pill?"

"No." Her eyes went wide. "There's been no reason. I don't date. But you had a condom."

"Yeah." One that was way past the expiration date.

It both pleased and disturbed him that she wasn't with another guy now and hadn't been for a while. But he'd been thinking with every part of his body except his head, and the only protection he had with him was aged, and not in a good way.

"It broke," he said.

"Thanks for telling me." She nodded thoughtfully. "I'm sure it won't be a problem. Don't you worry."

Yeah, he thought. That would happen.

Chapter Three

It was almost quitting time on Monday, and Ellie had never been so glad. She was exhausted from work, but mostly it was the strain of trying to act normal with Alex. How did you undo sex? How did you stop picturing your coworker naked when you'd actually seen him that way?

Good Lord, she'd slept with him but that wasn't even the worst. The next morning they'd had a discussion about why it couldn't happen again, all while still in his bed. How did a woman go to work and pretend it never happened when he was sitting at a desk just across the room?

Every time she looked at his brown bedroom eyes and broad shoulders, sex was all she could think about.

"The plumbing subcontractor will be here in the morning." Alex looked up and caught her staring. His eyes narrowed with something dark and intense, as if he knew what she'd been thinking.

"Right." The single word was almost a croak so she

swallowed, trying to stay loose. Fat chance. Her stomach clenched and her chest felt tight. "You're sure this is a good crew?"

"The best."

"Good. I'm not worried about the public areas which they could probably do in their sleep. It's the lines for the outpatient surgery and recovery rooms that make me nervous. We're talking a delivery system for oxygen and nitrous oxide used for anesthesia."

"These guys can handle it," he said confidently.

He was confident about everything, even making love to a woman. Darn it. There she went again. Time to get out of here. "I'm going to look things over and make sure we're good to go tomorrow before I leave for the day."

"Which you're planning to do soon, right? Leave for the day, I mean."

"Yes." Then she wondered if he was trying to get rid of her. "Why?"

"You look tired."

The man was too perceptive. Her bad was wondering if that meant he cared. She wasn't going to be one of those women who expected a man to have deeper feelings just because they'd slept together. Sex was a physical act between a man and a woman who found each other attractive. That's all it had been or ever would be.

"I've been putting in a lot of hours." She stood and closed her laptop. "But if I'd wanted a nine-to-five job, I'd have picked another profession."

"That wasn't criticism." Alex stood, too. "I just wanted to run something by you while you're doing the last inspection of the day, but if you're too tired it can wait."

"I'm fine. What is it?"

"I've been thinking about when we join the new part of the building with the clinic, and I think it's going to require a special expansion joint along with a new reglet cut into the existing wall."

She'd been thinking about that herself and knew he wanted the reglet, a flat, narrow architectural molding, to make the joining of the two structures strong and seamless. "Y'all think it won't hold up otherwise?"

"That's right." He walked out from behind his desk and stopped halfway to hers. "I'll show you what I mean, then you should go home."

"Okay."

By this time of day Ellie looked forward to kicking off her high heels. But when she met Alex in the middle of the room she was glad to have the extra height because of a weird, vulnerable feeling. Not about the work. He wasn't one of those jerks who figured she didn't know her eyebrow brush from an air duct. This was personal, and for some reason unclear to her at this moment, it was important to stand as tall as possible beside him.

"Okay. Let's do this and get you the heck out of here." He stepped in front of her and led the way, which was something he hadn't done since the day she'd arrived.

After opening the door he walked outside and held it for her before descending the three metal stairs. All day when he'd turned his back, her gaze had been drawn to his outstanding butt and now was no exception. Alex McKnight was a good-looking man in or out of his jeans. Maybe if she'd never seen him naked…

She was looking at his backside instead of the last step and her heel caught. One second she was upright and the next she went down with a small scream. Her body twisted to the side but her shoe didn't and she felt more than heard something in her ankle pop. Then a blinding pain ripped through her lower leg.

Alex was beside her instantly, one knee on the ground. "Are you okay?"

"I'm not sure. I think I twisted my ankle. It really hurts."

When he freed her high heel she cried out. "Dammit. I'm sorry."

"It's okay. Oh…gosh, that hurts. Can you help me up?"

His mouth pulled tight as he slid an arm around her waist and took her weight to get her standing. When she set her foot on the blacktop parking lot, she cried out again. The pain took her breath away.

"That's it." Alex scooped her into his arms. "Good thing there's a doctor right next door."

"That's not necessary. I'm sure it's just a sprain." Please, God.

"My brother can deal with that, too," he said grimly.

"You're sure I can't talk you out of this?"

"Not a chance in hell."

Truthfully, Ellie was glad he took over. She put her arms around his neck and gritted her teeth against the pain. Somewhere she'd heard that damage to the tendons and ligaments was painful and took longer to heal than a broken bone, but that seemed less incapacitating than the alternative. She couldn't be incapacitated. That would mean a delay in the Mercy Medical Clinic project. Delays were never good, but she couldn't afford one now while she was trying to reverse a black eye to her professional reputation.

Ellie was stretched out on the exam table at the clinic with her ankle elevated. She was waiting for the orthopedic specialist to return with the verdict—sprain or break. Dr. McKnight—he'd said to call him Ben—had told her it was probably broken, but the X-rays would tell definitively. After giving her something for the pain, he'd told her to rest. If only…

She'd never been so tired in her life. The pressure to be perfect on this job had taken a toll, and then there was Alex. Why couldn't he have been a sixty-year-old hunchback who looked like a troll? She could work with a troll, and a gnarled little man probably wouldn't have an award-winning butt capable of distracting a woman into falling down the stairs. Right this minute it was a toss-up about which was worse—pain or humiliation. Since the meds were working, she'd go with the latter for now.

When there was a soft knock on the exam room door, she carefully rolled to her side toward it, making the paper beneath her crinkle loudly. "Come in."

A second later Ginny Irwin stood in the doorway. "How are you feeling, sweetie?" The nurse's voice was firm and straightforward but not unkind.

"Better." Ellie shifted on the table and winced at the dull pain radiating from ankle to thigh. "I'm sure it's just a sprain."

Ginny was sixtyish and tall, her gray hair cut in a pixie style. Pity mixed with the no-nonsense expression in her blue eyes. "Sometimes the worst of it is not knowing. Can't take action until you know what action to take."

"Do you have any idea when the doctor will get the results of the X-rays?"

"I wish. We shoot the pictures, but a trained radiologist has to read them. In a perfect world there would be one available to interpret the films, but you're in Blackwater Lake. The good news is you have Ben McKnight."

"Oh?" And she'd slept with his brother. Would he hold that against her if he knew?

Ginny moved beside the table. "If this happened in Dallas you couldn't have a better orthopedic specialist. I've never seen him call an X-ray wrong."

"So he can tell me whether or not it's broken—"

"'Fraid not, sweetie. In his opinion that would be making a guess, since that's not his specialty." Ginny pressed index and middle fingers to Ellie's wrist, presumably taking a pulse. She nodded with satisfaction. "The films we took are remotely read. They're emailed to the hospital, where the radiologist will make the determination and give Ben a report. There's no telling how long it will be before we have the results."

Ellie felt a little spurt of panic. "What happens if it gets too late?"

"Don't borrow trouble," the nurse advised. "We'll cross that bridge when and if we have to. Here at Mercy Medical Clinic we're good at improvising."

"I didn't mean to be pushy. No offense meant."

"None taken. You're hurting and handling it much better than some. It's human nature when you're in pain and scared to lash out. You're impatient." Ginny grinned. "No pun intended. I can handle that. It's perfectly natural to wonder what's going to happen."

"I'll try not to be too antsy."

"Not on my account." The older woman studied her with a critical eye. "Can I get you something? A snack? We've got cookies and fruit in the break room. Maybe something to drink? Ginger ale to give you something to keep up your strength?"

"No, thanks." Her stomach was tied in knots. "I don't think I could get anything down right now."

"Yes, you can. I know just the thing." Without waiting for a protest Ginny turned to leave. "Now you try to rest."

Easier said than done, Ellie thought. She was feeling pathetically alone and abandoned when there was another knock on the door. She prayed it was Ben McKnight bearing good news.

"Come in."

A moment later there was a McKnight in the doorway but not the one she'd hoped to see.

Alex was holding a can of ginger ale and a plastic cup with a flex straw in it. "Hi."

Ellie was irritated that he could look so darn good when she felt like roadkill. "I told you to go home."

Those had been her exact words right after he'd carried her all the way from the construction trailer to this exam room in the clinic. And he'd handled her as if she weighed no more than a child. Now she sounded witchy and ungrateful.

"I appreciate all your help, Alex. I didn't mean to be rude."

He put the can down on the counter by the sink and popped the tab. "Is that a Texas thing?"

"What?"

"You worrying about my feelings when you've got to be hurting like hell."

"I was raised to have manners and to be kind and polite to everyone. And, just for the record, I don't *have* to be hurting. I'm sure it's just a sprain."

"Even if you're right, that doesn't mean you're not in pain. And if you want to take it out on me, go for it." He poured the fizzy soda into the cup and waited for the bubbles to go down before bringing it over to the exam table. "Now, take a sip."

"I told the nurse I didn't care for anything."

"There you go again with that well-bred, Southern fried stoic stuff. You don't have energy to spare for manners, so cut yourself some slack. Now drink some of this. You've been through a trauma." He must have seen the stubborn trickling through her, because he added, "I was told to make myself useful and give you liquids, and that's what I intend to do. Ginny Irwin scares the crap out of me and everyone else in Blackwater Lake who comes here to Mercy Medical for treatment. If you're as smart as I think you are, you'll be scared of her, too, and do what you're told."

Ellie didn't think anything or anyone could have made her even want to smile, but Alex and what he'd just said proved her wrong. She raised up on an elbow. "Okay. Since you put it that way…"

He held out the glass and steadied the straw while she drank. "That's a good girl."

After getting about half of it down, she stretched out on her side again and gingerly adjusted her injured leg. Strangely enough, she did feel a little better. "Thank you."

"You're welcome." He scanned her from face to feet. "How do you feel?"

"How do I look?" The way his mouth pulled tight wasn't very reassuring. "Tell me the truth."

"Your face is white as a sheet and your ankle is swollen. A lot."

"I appreciate your candor." And she sincerely meant that. Honesty was very important to her, but it didn't make the increasingly panicked feeling go away.

"Everything will be okay, Ellie."

How will everything be all right? she wanted to ask. A broken ankle would slow her down. It wasn't in her comeback plan or her schedule. She'd already lost too much time with that darn, stupid emotional detour on the road to professional success. There wasn't any flexibility in her blueprint to rehabilitate her reputation and resurrect her career.

"I have no doubt that things will work out." She was

pretty sure the words had just enough confidence to be convincing.

"Darn right. Whatever happens, if you need anything, just ask."

Not going there, she thought. She'd trusted a man once, and it hadn't gone well. She would get through this on her own. What didn't kill you made you stronger.

"I'm sure I won't need anything, Alex, but the offer is awfully nice." She smiled as sincerely as possible. "It's way past quitting time. Y'all should head home."

"I'm in no hurry."

That made one of them. She was in a huge hurry for him to take his care and concern out of here before she started to believe in it.

"Really," she said. "I'm okay. There's no reason to waste any more of your evening on me."

"I don't mind—"

A knock interrupted him just before the door opened. Ben came in with X-rays in his hand. "Hey, Alex. I didn't know you were still here."

"I was just telling him he should go," Ellie said.

The doctor looked at her. "I've got the radiologist report."

"Finally." Now that it was here she was dreading the results.

The two brothers stood side by side, and the family resemblance was obvious. The shapes of their faces were identical right down to the strong chin and rugged cheekbones. Their coloring was slightly different; the doctor's hair was lighter. Alex was just a shade taller, broader in the shoulders. His hair was darker, his brown eyes more intense. When he made no move to leave, Ben cleared his voice.

"Obviously you two are friends, but I need to talk to Ellie privately. It's a patient confidentiality issue."

"Oh. Right. Sorry." Alex set the plastic glass and straw on the counter beside the soda can and left the room.

When the door closed behind him, Ellie didn't know whether to be relieved that he'd listened to his brother or to miss his reassuring support. But this mess wasn't his baby to rock.

"Okay, then. What's up, Doc?"

He shoved the X-ray films on the viewer box and even the untrained eye could see the bones of the foot, ankle and lower leg. Using his pen as a pointer he indicated an irregularity.

"I'm sorry, Ellie. I know you were hoping it was just a sprain, but that's not the case. There's definitely a fracture here."

"Okay." She took a deep but not very calming breath. "So what now? You put it in a cast. Maybe the walking kind," she said hopefully. "So I can get back to work."

"I'll put a cast on it so you don't make the injury worse while we wait for the swelling to go down."

She didn't like the sound of that. "What happens then?"

"I need to do the repair in surgery. It will require a plate to hold the bone together while it heals. But here's the thing…"

"What?" The knots in her stomach pulled tighter.

"When the clinic addition is finished, a procedure like this can be done here, on an outpatient basis, but you can't wait that long. We need the hospital and it's pretty far away."

Close to that cute little airport where she'd flown in from Dallas. "How much work time will I lose?"

"The day of the surgery, then one or two after because there might be some discomfort from the procedure."

"And can I work in the meantime?"

"Yes, if you can do what you need to on crutches. You can't put any weight on the leg, and common sense is essential. Keep the foot elevated as much as possible to get the swelling down. The sooner the surgery is done, the sooner you'll be back on your feet."

"Okay."

"Do you have any other questions?" There was sympathy in the doctor's dark eyes.

"Not right now, but I'm sure I will."

"When you do, don't hesitate to ask."

She nodded numbly.

Ellie figured she was in shock. It was the only explanation for her state of calm through the process of getting the cast on. When it was done, Ginny gave her crutches and instructions, then helped her into a wheelchair. She was on her way to the clinic waiting area and about to ask the nurse for the favor of a bit longer ride to her car in the lot by the construction trailer. Before getting the words out, she spotted Alex sitting in a chair.

Ginny wheeled her closer and said to him, "Here she is."

"Thanks, Ginny."

Ellie heard the squeak of the woman's sneakers on the wooden floor behind her as she walked away. She couldn't believe he was still there. More important, she didn't want to get used to it.

She shook her head. "You shouldn't be here."

Chapter Four

Alex was reminded of an angry, scared hummingbird when he looked at Ellie Hart. She was in a wheelchair, holding a pair of crutches and wearing a hot-pink cast that came to just below the knee on her left leg. He was pond scum for thinking she made a broken ankle look sexy, but a man couldn't necessarily control the direction of his thoughts when a crisis was over. Now that they were in stable mode, he needed to focus on the situation at hand, which was that she didn't particularly want him here.

"You should know something about me, Ellie."

"What's that?"

"I don't always do what I'm told."

"Why doesn't that surprise me?" The attempt at humor didn't ease the tension in her shoulders.

"This time I have a good reason."

"And that is?" Her chin lifted a notch as if she were preparing for battle.

"You're my architect." He experienced a momentary stab of possessiveness that had nothing to do with business. "The state of your health could potentially affect Mercy Medical Clinic's expansion deadline and I can't afford not to meet it."

"Neither can I." Her full lips pressed together and it wasn't about pain, at least not the physical kind. "I studied hard and worked even harder and messed up my first chance to establish my name in the business. This opportunity is about digging my reputation out of a very deep hole. If it doesn't come in on time and within budget, I'll have a better chance of flapping my arms and flying to the moon than having an actual career as an architect."

"So, about that medical confidentiality thing…" He dragged his fingers through his hair as their gazes met. "Do you want to tell me what my brother said?"

"Not really." The determination in her eyes told him that was true enough, but there was vulnerability, too. She blew out a breath. "But y'all have a right to know. There's no way to sugarcoat this. My ankle is broken."

"Oh, Ellie— I'm sorry. I know you were hoping for different news."

She tried to shrug it off, but the shadows leaked through. "You play the hand you're dealt, as Hastings Hart would say."

Alex had a feeling her daddy held his daughter to a high standard and she was an overachiever. "Okay. It's broken, but not the end of the world. We can work with that. Now you're in a cast and one assumes since you have crutches there won't be a marathon in your near future. This setback will only slow you down some."

"It's not that simple."

"Why?"

"Ben says I need surgery. He has to line up the bones

then put a plate in to keep them that way so it will heal correctly. Otherwise I won't be running a marathon ever, or walking, either, for that matter. That will make it kind of hard to navigate a job site under my own power. And it can't wait until the clinic expansion is finished."

"Okay." Alex rested his elbows on his knees as he thought that one over. "So you get the surgery done ASAP."

"I have to wait until the swelling goes down. Then it means a trip to the hospital, which isn't just around the corner. But it won't be overnight. I can have it done on an outpatient basis."

"Okay. That officially sucks," he agreed. "But we can spare you at the job site when you need to take the time. This isn't a disaster." He noticed that the polish on her toes matched the hot-pink cast and was possibly one of the most erotic things he'd ever seen. "Except for you, of course."

"No kidding." She sighed. "This is most definitely not my finest hour."

"Are you in pain?"

"It aches some because what they gave me here has worn off. But I'm tough." She looked anything but. More like an abandoned kitten. "Ben said over-the-counter pain medication should do the trick if I'm uncomfortable."

"Okay, then. I'll drive you—"

She shook her head. "Not necessary. I can do it. The injury is to my left ankle, so I can drive."

"I'm sure you can, Ellie, but I'm here and you don't have to. I'll take you wherever you want to go."

"I want to go home, but there's no need for y'all to go out of the way."

"It's not really. I live near the lake, not far from the apartment you're renting." A thought struck him. "Don't you live upstairs?"

"I do." She looked a little worried about that before her

stubborn side kicked in and shut it down. "I'll manage. Y'all shouldn't give it another thought."

"How?"

"I'm sorry?"

"How will you manage to get yourself up the stairs?"

"I just will. Don't trouble yourself about me." It cost her reserves of energy that she probably didn't have, but she managed to smile. "Now, it's been a real exciting day and I'm ready to call it a night. I'll just say goodbye and thank you. I'm sure the nurse will help me out to my car."

She set the rubber-tipped crutches on the floor and hauled herself to a standing position with the curved, padded part under her arms. Her humongous purse was hanging from one of the wheelchair's handles, and Alex could see that she was trying to figure out how to manage it.

"Let me," he said, surging to his feet.

"It's not necessary. I should get used to doing this for myself."

"Yes, you should. But not tonight." When she opened her mouth to protest he snapped, "Stuff a sock in it, Ellie. I wasn't raised by wolves. There's no need to bother Ginny. I'm right here and I'll see you to your car."

The expression in her eyes said she wanted to talk him out of that, but she must have been a quart low on spunk because she nodded. "Thanks."

"Don't mention it."

Alex had once broken his leg playing high school football. The experience had taught him that no matter how athletic a person was, it took time and practice to get the hang of crutches. After saying goodbye to Ginny and Ben, he carried her big bag and held the clinic door open so Ellie could get out. The trip from there to the construction parking area was excruciatingly slow and painful if the tightness of her mouth was anything to go by.

He wanted to haul her into his arms and carry her, but it wasn't just about speeding up the process or minimizing her discomfort. As hard as he tried, he couldn't seem to forget how good holding her had felt that night on his boat. Granted she'd been naked, but her cute, curvy little self even when wearing clothes was pure, one hundred percent temptation.

That thought made him break out in a sweat, though the June evening was cool. The sweet sexy scent of her skin drifted on the breeze and slid through him, then floated around in his belly where it finally knotted and settled in. He swore that a lifetime and a half passed before they got to her car. Fishing her keys out of that gigantic purse was nearly as hard as resisting her. It wouldn't have surprised him if all her worldly possessions were in the bag.

He unlocked the driver's door and said, "Are you sure about this?"

"Very." Awkwardly she maneuvered herself to the opening.

Alex could almost see her mind working to figure out the logistics. "Back yourself in and slowly lower your butt to the seat." An erotic image of him squeezing that soft sweet body part flashed through his mind and he gritted his teeth. "Then sit down and hand the crutches to me."

She seemed to be thinking through that advice, then successfully did as he said. "Okay. Thanks."

"I'm going to put these on the front passenger side so they're handy. It will take some eye-hand coordination, but you'll be able to get them into place for standing. Just swing your legs out and pull yourself up."

"Okay. Got it."

He still couldn't see how she was going to get herself up the stairs in her current condition, but the lady seemed determined to do it alone, and he knew he should be grateful for her independence. When the crutches were stowed within reach, he leaned down in the open doorway and looked at her in the driver's seat. "If you need anything at all, you call me."

"Thanks. I'll be fine and dandy. You'll see."

Yes he would, and sooner than she realized. Because as hard as he tried, he just couldn't trust that independent streak of hers.

Alex closed the door and stood back while she started the car then pulled slowly onto Main Street. In seconds she was out of sight, but nowhere near out of his mind.

He'd come this close to pulling Ellie into his arms and holding her for a very long time. How stupid was that? Not only was she dealing with a broken ankle, they'd agreed that sleeping together was a mistake that shouldn't and wouldn't happen again.

It was just that she tugged at him. Her spunky, self-reliant streak made him want to be there for her. But someone had made her believe there was shame in asking for help. Could have been the jerk who lied to her and cost her a career start. Or it could have been the way she was raised. He wanted five minutes alone, no questions asked, with whoever had drilled that lesson into her. She didn't have to do this alone.

And he was going to prove it to her whether she wanted to know or not.

The drive from the town of Blackwater Lake to the lake itself was only a couple of miles but turned into the longest of Ellie's life. Although she'd had a license for years, it felt like her first time behind the wheel. That actually was the case, since this was her first time driving with a broken left ankle. She used her good foot to press the gas and brake pedals, but even it felt heavy. The injury somehow threw off her timing, but she made the trip in one piece.

And that was when her problems really started.

After parking in her assigned space, she saw that Adam Stone's car wasn't there, because he and his bride were on their honeymoon. Then she opened her driver's door and grabbed one of the crutches to get herself out. Because the interior was compact and the thing was unwieldy, it was impossible to maneuver, and she kept getting hung up on the dashboard, windshield or steering wheel.

"Now what?" She was frustrated and close to tears. "You can do this, Ellie. You're a Hart and an architect. There's no crying in this big girl world. Pull yourself together. You are woman. W-o-m-a-n. Roar, girl."

She thought for a moment, then decided they would probably come out the same way Alex had put them in. From the outside. The only challenge would be doing it on one leg, but she could hop around to the other side and use the car for support.

It worked, but even though she didn't put weight on the leg, the jarring movement sent shards of pain through her ankle, and she was sweating by the time she'd braced the crutches under her arms. Her gaze landed on the purse in the passenger seat. There was no way she could balance and walk with the monstrosity on her shoulder, so she hung it around her neck.

Like the drive out here, it took a while to get to the front porch where the outside light was on, and she began to really regret not letting Alex help out. There were three steps up before even starting on the stairs to her apartment. Just hopping around the car had nearly brought her down—this was really going to be a challenge.

Longingly she looked at the rocking chair beside Adam and Jill's door. A small table stood beside it, perfect for elevating her injured leg if she could figure out how to get there.

Holding the crutches in one hand and the railing with the other and her purse still around her neck, she braced for the pain and hopped up one step. It was a miracle she kept herself from falling. The handbag felt as if the entire state of Texas was inside. All she needed was to break something else. Steadying herself, she went through the process two more times and leaned heavily on the post supporting the porch roof.

"Thank God." She made it to the rocker and dropped into it. After resting for a minute she pulled the small round table toward her and lifted her injured leg on it. "That's as elevated as I can get it."

The hard, sad truth was sinking in fast. She might get up the stairs to her apartment, but by the time she did it would be time to go to work in the morning. She had to find somewhere else to stay for the night either on the ground floor or with elevator access, and Blackwater Lake Lodge was the only game in town.

After pulling out her cell phone she called information and agreed to the direct connection fee. After two rings the call was answered.

"Blackwater Lake Lodge. This is M.J. How may I help you?"

"Hi, M.J. My name is Ellie Hart—"

"You're the architect for the Mercy Medical Clinic expansion project."

"Yes, I am." Wow, word traveled fast in a small town.

"Is everything all right?"

No, but she wondered about the question. "Why do you ask?"

"Well, the only reason you'd be calling the lodge is for

a room, but I thought you were staying in Jill Beck's—I mean Jill Stone's—apartment."

Wow again. People knew your business here. "I am. And you're correct. Everything isn't all right. I had a little accident."

"I hope it's not too serious."

"No. I'll be fine. But there's a cast on my leg. And the apartment is upstairs, which I can't manage right now. I was wondering if there might be something available at the lodge."

"I'm so sorry, Ellie. We're completely full." M.J. sounded really, sincerely sorry. "Is there anything I can do? Someone I can call for you?"

Alex was her first thought, but that bridge was burned. "You're sure there's nothing even for one or two nights while I figure all this out?"

"I'm looking." The sound of clicking on a keyboard came through loud and clear. Then apology wrapped around the words when she said, "I feel just awful, but we're all booked. In fact, there's a waiting list. Let me make some calls and I'll see if I can find a room for you—"

"That's very sweet, but I can't ask you to do that. You're working. I'll find something."

"You're sure?"

"Absolutely. I'll call Brenda Miller. She's one of the carpenters on the construction crew. We've gotten to know each other." They said good morning every day. "Thanks, anyway, M.J."

"I don't know her, but good luck. And if she can't help call me back. I mean it."

"I'll do that. Thanks."

Ellie clicked the phone closed and leaned back on the wooden headrest. She was so tired and sore that crying was sounding better and better all the time, so she let her eyes drift closed to keep back the tears. It seemed like seconds later she heard her name.

"Ellie. Wake up." The masculine voice was soft, gentle, yet deep and familiar.

She blinked her eyes open and Alex was crouched in front of her. "Where am I?"

"On Jill's porch. Downstairs from your apartment."

The horrible truth came rushing back and she nodded. Her mouth quivered when she said, "I can't get up the stairs. And don't you dare say I told you so."

"Never crossed my mind." But he looked away to keep her from seeing the truth in his eyes.

"I called the lodge but they don't have a room available even for just tonight. But I have a plan."

"Does it include sleeping here outside on the porch?"

"No," she said, struggling for a tone of confident superiority. "There's a roof and four walls."

His eyes narrowed. "How about lights and running water?"

"That, too."

"Care to share the location?" When she hesitated he added, "I'll find out, anyway. I followed you here and it's real easy to do it again."

She was torn between a spurt of happiness that he'd gone to the trouble of checking up on her and not wanting to appear vulnerable. Since he seemed determined, coming clean was her only option.

"I'm going to stay in the construction trailer."

He shook his head. "Bad idea."

"It will work," she snapped. Anger would keep her from crying, but changing the subject would be better. "Why did you follow me?"

"Apparently I'm coming to your rescue."

"That would imply I'm in trouble and that's just not the case."

The corners of his mouth curved up. "Let me get this straight. Your ankle is broken. The leg is in a cast and doctor's orders are not to put weight on it. On top of that, the apartment you rent and where you keep all your stuff is up a flight of stairs that you can't climb. There's no room at the lodge and your plan is to stay at a flimsy trailer with no bed and a bathroom with only a sink. Do I have that right?"

Unfortunately he'd hit on every single depressing detail. "It will be fine."

He rested his forearms on his thighs as they stared eye to eye. It didn't look as if he was leaving anytime soon. "Is everyone from Texas as stubborn as you?"

"I can't speak for everyone, but there was a time when Texans wanted to form their own country. To this day there are holdouts for that idea."

"I think I can guess where you fall on the issue." He looked down for a moment then reluctantly seemed to make up his mind. "You're coming home with me."

She'd slept with him, and they'd agreed it was a mistake. Now he was suggesting she live with him in his house? That suggestion was worse than bad, but she couldn't think of a word bad enough to describe it, except possibly *disastrous*.

"That's not a good idea."

"Maybe. But I don't see another alternative." When she opened her mouth to protest, he held up a finger to stop her. "The construction trailer isn't a realistic, long-term option. There's no bed or shower. Not to mention it's a place of business no matter how temporary."

There must be another solution. She'd crossed a line with him that night on his boat and keeping her distance was the only way to get back neutral territory.

"Alex, I can't let you do this."

He dragged his fingers through his hair and if the irritation darkening his face was an indication, he wasn't any happier about this than she was.

"As I see it," he said, "there's no other choice. For either of us. The work comes first. You've got skin in the game and so do I. Delays aren't an option."

"Why? I mean I know for myself, but what's in it for you?"

"I fit this project into a small window as a favor to Mayor Goodson and the town council, but there's very little room for error. I've got a big development job scheduled to start. The guy's worth a bundle and has something of a reputation."

"In what way?"

"Wealthy bachelor."

"A player?"

"Maybe. But he generates a lot of publicity, and I'd prefer it not be bad when my company is mentioned. It's a very lucrative deal."

"I see." In the short term she didn't have much money on the line, but this was about her long-term career.

There was determination in Alex's gaze. "If you don't show up at the job site there's too much potential for delays and work stoppage. My offer of a place to stay is all about keeping this project on schedule. Nothing more."

Ellie should have been relieved and she would be. Real soon. But she couldn't manage it just now. The fact that she was even the tiniest bit disappointed that he had only professional motivation for offering her a roof over her head meant that her feelings for him were a little too personal. On the other hand, she had no choice.

"Okay, Alex. I accept. And it's very nice of you."

"Like I said, I'm not a nice man."

There was something hot, hard and a little primitive in his eyes that said he wasn't being chivalrous and she shouldn't believe for a second that he was. The little thrill feathering through her proved that she didn't quite buy in to that. He had the look down, but she wondered if it was an act. Or simply a habit to warn women away.

He didn't scare her. She had skin in the professional game, too, and didn't do personal any more than he did.

"I really hate to ask, but I'm going to need some things from upstairs. I would do it if I could, but I think I'm going to have to impose on you. Unless you can think of another way."

He thought for several moments, then seemed to conclude that lugging her upstairs, back down again and making another trip for her stuff was not the most efficient way to achieve the goal.

"I'll get it. What do you need?"

She started talking as items popped into her mind. "Toiletries. Clothes. Underwear."

It was hard to tell in the dim light, but she swore he went a little pale. She wasn't sure whether or not to take satisfaction from that.

Chapter Five

As soon as Alex stepped into Ellie's upstairs apartment he realized how big a mistake he'd made. This whole place smelled like her, all flowers and spice and everything nice. One sniff and his hands tingled with the need to touch her. Chances were pretty damn good that she would leave her scent all over his house and there'd be absolutely nowhere to hide. Since he'd actually put some effort into convincing her to come home with him, she would notice if he tried to get out of it now. That meant he was pretty seriously hosed.

All he could do was get this part done and deal with the fallout from his big mouth later. He pulled his cell phone from the case on his belt and hit speed dial for Ellie's number. She was going to talk him through and tell him what to get.

"Hi, Alex."

That was probably exhaustion in her voice but it sounded

all husky and honey to him. "Where's your suitcase?" he asked, not bothering to be polite.

"Bedroom closet."

He walked past the leather couch in the living room and went down the hall. As he passed the bathroom, her scent became even stronger, but he planned to get busy and do his best to ignore the way his senses were scrambling.

"Okay, I found it," he said, looking into her closet.

The interior highlighted her temporary status. This was practically empty compared to the ones he'd seen when invited into a woman's bedroom during one of his out-of-town trips. Ellie had a couple of suits with matching four-inch heels that she wouldn't be wearing any time soon. There were black slacks, silky blouses and a couple of flowing skirts. And some straight, tight ones, too.

"With that cast of yours, you're probably better off with skirts. The loose ones."

"Yeah," she said. "And there's a pair of white tennis shoes. They'll have to do for now."

"Should I just put in the right one?"

"Funny." She sighed. "Humor me and bring the pair."

"Okay. Got 'em."

"Bring the shorts in the middle drawer and the sweatpants. Three, I think. If I have to cut off the legs it's not a big loss."

In the dresser he located the items. "They're in. What else?"

"Underwear and bras." Her tone was matter-of-fact, but she was working at it. "Top drawer."

Alex opened it and started to sweat. Pink, yellow, green, red and black. It was a relentlessly feminine rainbow of matching panties and bras, each color sexier than the last. Tiny little bikini panties made of silk and satin trimmed with lace. They would be cut high and make her legs look longer....

"You want all of them?" He hoped his voice didn't sound as hoarse to her as it did to him.

"Yes."

"Okay." His tone was offhanded, too, but barely.

His hand shook when he picked up all the scraps of female apparel. Taking lingerie off a woman was a major turn-on. That was a given for a guy, but putting it in a suitcase shouldn't rev his motor like this. Except damned if she didn't have just about the sexiest underwear on the planet.

"What else?" he barked into the cell phone.

"Nightgown and pajamas."

He almost groaned out loud but just managed to hold it in. "Dresser?"

"Bottom drawer."

Alex was almost afraid to open it. After silk and lace what were the odds that she wore sensible stuff to bed like flannel or a big, baggy shirt with enough space to completely hide her tempting curves? The first cautious glance was like peeking into his own personal hell. Skimpy, skinny-strapped tops that wouldn't conceal diddly and little matching bottoms so short they'd barely cover the mind-blowing curve of her bottom. Not giving himself too much time to think, he scooped everything out and dropped it in the suitcase.

As if she could read his mind, Ellie said, "There's a robe hanging on the back of the bathroom door."

He found it and breathed a sigh of relief. Terry cloth, thick and long. "Thank you, God."

"What was that?" she asked.

"Think I got everything," he answered.

"Don't forget the toiletries."

"What are we talking?"

"Shampoo, conditioner, detangler, volumizer, stuff for shine, hair spray. Makeup. The little machine and charger I use to cleanse my face. Body cream—"

"You're kidding, right?"

"You think looking this good is fast, easy and cheap?" she snapped.

He thought she was beautiful first thing in the morning with mascara under her eyes and her hair tousled because he'd run his hands through it. None of that would come out of his mouth, though.

"What I think," he said carefully, "is that I'll bring down your clothes and put them in the truck then come back up for the rest. This is a two-trip proposition."

There was silence on the other end of the line for several moments. "I'm sorry, Alex. I'll understand if you want to take back your offer."

He did, but not for the reason she thought. "I don't go back on my word. Be down in a minute."

After zipping shut the suitcase, he grabbed the clothes on hangers, then went downstairs. Ellie was still in the rocker with her bad leg elevated. She was leaning back with her eyes closed, which was both good news and bad. When she was looking at him straight on with those big blue eyes, there was extreme danger of falling into the pit, with nothing to grab hold of.

But now he could see the dark circles under her eyes and the paleness of her cheeks that hinted at the discomfort she was doing her best to hide. That made him a slug for thinking what he'd thought about her underthings.

"Thank you," she said quietly, staring at him. "I really hate being a bother."

"Don't mention it." There was a noticeable tug on his heart at her words. "Did I mention that my house is one story, so there are no stairs involved? And I have a house-keeper."

"I'm sure she'll love the extra work."

"Martha is all bark and no bite."

"What we in Texas call 'all hat and no saddle'?"

He couldn't help smiling. "Something like that. She'll love having a woman around."

"I'll do my best to reduce any evidence of my presence in your home."

"Okay, then. I'll finish this up."

He tucked away the first load of her things then went back upstairs for the rest. After stashing that, too, he walked up the three steps to the porch. She reached for the crutches and he gently brushed away her hand.

"I'll give you a ride."

Without waiting for protest, he scooped her up and carried her to the open door on the passenger side, then set her on the leather seat. All her tempting curves were a heavy weight in his mind but not so much in his arms. The feel of her made the packing challenge seem like a cold shower.

The sooner he got her to his house, the sooner he could retire to his corner and get at least a little distance from her. He walked around the front of the truck, then got in behind the wheel and turned the key in the ignition.

Ellie leaned her head back against the seat and sighed. "I'm not quite sure how to manage it, but all I want is a hot shower and to wash my hair."

Alex couldn't decide whether she could read his mind or was just really good at torturing him. "Correct me if I'm wrong, but aren't you supposed to keep that cast dry? Maybe you could figure out something slightly less challenging than washing your hair."

"I can handle it."

He couldn't. "The thing is, I'd rather not have to call

my brother in the middle of the night because your new plaster accessory was compromised on my watch."

"Are you afraid of Ben?"

"Of course not." He was afraid she'd hurt herself more and that bothered him a lot. "How about this. Give me a day and I'll change out the showerhead in the guest bath and put in a handheld one. That way you can control the flow and direction of the water."

"You shouldn't have to make any changes to your home on account of me, Alex."

"It's not for you." That was only a small lie. "And I've been meaning to do it for a while."

"That's very sweet." There was a soft look on her face in the dim dashboard lights.

"Odd. Because I'm not a sweet guy."

"Oh, please." She laughed. "I don't want to be a bother. If you're sure…"

Since the day he met her, Alex hadn't been sure about anything and she'd been a bother in ways he didn't want to think about. "I'm sure, and it's no trouble."

"Okay, then. Thanks."

She was quiet for the rest of the drive, but that didn't make any difference to the tension knotting his shoulders and neck. Finally the turn for his place came up. He went right and drove down the long driveway. "We're almost there."

"You do live close," she said.

Alex parked in front of his house with the impressive stately entrance and double doors containing etched-glass inserts that let the inside light spill out. He told her to sit tight while he unlocked and opened the front door.

When he came back to the truck and moved in close to her he said, "Here's how we're doing this. I'll carry you into the family room, and you stay put while I bring the rest of your stuff in."

"Only if you let me unpack everything. I can handle that."

"Okay."

He was grateful not to touch it again, but that wouldn't keep him from remembering the look, the feel. Only feeling that silk on her body would be worse. There was no comfort in the fact that it wouldn't stay on her body for long.

"On second thought," she said, "if you put me and the toiletries in the guest bath, I can sit and arrange it all."

He thought that over and couldn't see a downside. "Sounds like a plan."

Alex carried her through the one-story house for a guided tour. He showed her the guest room and bath, his study and the master bedroom, then left her and the personal products where she could unpack them while he unloaded everything else and took it into the room where she would sleep.

Ten minutes later he stood in the bathroom doorway, where the scent of her was already taking over. The thick terry-cloth robe was in his hand. "I'll just hang this on the back of the door. Towels and washcloths are in the linen closet there, and I put a fresh bar of soap in the shower if you need it."

"Thanks." She smiled. "I really mean that."

"Happy to be of service." He slid his fingers into the pockets of his jeans. "If you need some help, I'd be happy to stay. Promise not to look."

"As if." But she laughed and the sweet sound was almost as powerful as the smell of her skin.

"Okay, I'm leaving. But I'll be close by." He closed the door and stayed right outside in the hall. Balancing on one leg was new to her, and if she had a problem, he wanted to be close.

There was no noise for a while, then he heard running water. After a few minutes, it shut off and something fell on the floor. He tensed, waiting for some indication that Ellie was in distress. Although he was listening intently, a loud crash on the other side of the door was startling.

"Ellie, are you okay?" He knocked and heard mumbling but nothing else. That wasn't good enough. Just hours ago he'd seen her on the ground writhing in pain and couldn't stand the thought that it was happening again. "Ready or not, I'm coming in."

He burst through the door expecting the worst. And he got it, although not exactly as he'd expected. She was standing by the tub/shower with one hand on the wall to steady her and keep the weight off the broken ankle. That was the good part. The bad was that she had nothing on except a towel.

Tanned legs, toned arms, tempting cleavage were all in plain view. He could only imagine the stuff he couldn't see under that thick terry cloth, which he could get off her with just the flick of a wrist.

Bringing her here *was* a big mistake, but man, he was having a hell of a time remembering all the reasons why. Except one picture was worth a thousand words.

"Are you all right?"

No, I'm not all right, Ellie thought.

She was standing there in a towel, although that hardly mattered since he'd already seen her in nothing. But Alex was looking at her as if he could either kiss her or kill her and wasn't particularly choosy about which it would be. In the next instant he was undressing her with his eyes. She'd always thought that was a stupid expression, but right this second the meaning was completely clear and she didn't much mind. On top of that, his breathing was none too steady and that was making hers unsteady, too.

"I dropped the bottle of shampoo," she said, not really answering the question. "All I want to do is wash my hair, but the sink is too small and I can't bend over the tub."

"You're not hurt?" He dragged his fingers through his hair and his hand was shaky. "You didn't fall?"

"No. To both."

"You scared the hell out of me, Ellie."

"I'm sorry. It's just so darn frustrating. I can't move around normally. It's awkward. And my leg hurts."

"I know. It will take time to get used to this—"

"Don't patronize me. I couldn't wait for you to change the showerhead. All I want to do is wash my hair. It shouldn't be that hard. And now I'm repeating myself." She sighed. It wasn't fair to take this out on him. "Still, the rest of me is clean, so I'll live with the disappointment and figure it all out tomorrow."

His mouth pulled tight before he snapped, "Get dressed."

"Really? You're giving me orders now?" Self-righteous indignation would be easier to pull off if she wasn't standing on one leg while wearing only a towel.

"It's my house and I can say what I want. Concentrating on the current problem will be a lot easier if you're wearing some clothes."

"Oh." Wow. That was pretty cool that he was hot and bothered. Inconvenient, all things considered, but cool nonetheless.

"So, get dressed and meet me in the kitchen." He picked up the bottle of shampoo on the floor then walked out and closed the door.

Ellie was shaking, partly from the exertion of her physical limitations and partly her reaction to Alex's raw sexuality and the fact that he'd focused all of it on her. That wouldn't be a problem if she wasn't attracted to him, too.

"Stop it, Suellen Hart. Eyes on the prize."

She dropped the towel and managed to get her robe on then hopped out of the bathroom and into the guest suite. It was a really big, beautiful room with a queen-size bed and matching oak armoire. There was a dressing table with mirror and bench where she could sit and do hair and makeup. How she would have loved to wash her hair, but that wasn't a hill she'd die on tonight.

In spite of her vow to unpack for herself, Alex had done it. She found clean underthings and pulled out sweatpants that would fit over the cast and a T-shirt. After dressing, she found her way to the kitchen where Alex stood in front of the stainless-steel sink. His arms were folded over his chest, and he was looking very broody about something.

"Reporting for duty as ordered, sir." If not for the crutches, she'd have saluted like a smart aleck. They still felt clumsy, but she managed to clunk and swing herself to a place right in front of him. "So, why am I here?"

The bottle of shampoo was beside him along with a dark blue terry-cloth towel. "You want your hair washed."

"Everyone wants something they can't have."

"This isn't one of them. You can bend over the sink and I'll do the washing." He pointed to the nozzle that pulled out and had a hose attached.

"Y'all don't really have to do this. I promise not to blog or twitter about what a horrible host you are."

"Look—" There was a whole lot of irritation in that single word. "I'm not going to waste my breath trying to talk you into this. Do you want to wash your hair or not?"

"Yes." She moved closer before he changed his mind.

"Okay. This is how it will go. Brace yourself against

the sink, hunch your shoulders forward and hold on. I'll
do the rest."

"Got it."

She did as instructed and closed her eyes, then felt him
rake all her hair forward before the warm water wet it
down. The shampoo was cold until he massaged the blob
into fragrant, cleansing bubbles.

"That feels heavenly." The thought sort of slipped out
on a sigh and she really hoped he didn't hear. When there
was no comment, she figured the sound of the water had
concealed the words.

In a weird way this was more intimate and erotic than
being nearly naked in a towel. His body bumped and
brushed against hers because he had to get in close. She
felt his heat and innate confidence and strength in a way
she'd never felt a man's strength before. His fingers were
strong yet gentle as he stroked from the nape of her neck,
behind her ears and to her forehead. He washed longer
than was probably necessary but Ellie didn't mind. She
could have stayed like that forever. But finally he rinsed,
making sure all the soap was out. Conditioner would have
been nice, but it wasn't a good idea to push her luck.

When the water was off he said, "The towel is by your
right hand. I'll hold you steady while you put it around
your hair."

"Okay."

His hands were solid and steady at her waist as she
wrapped the towel into a turban on her head. Then he
helped turn her so they were face-to-face. She was ex-
traordinarily grateful for this gesture and wasn't sure what
to say.

"Thank you, Alex." The words didn't seem enough,
and she was just close enough to touch her lips to his
cheek. When she did, he tensed. "I really appreciate what

you did. It was above and beyond the call of duty. You're a very nice man."

He backed away as if she'd slapped him. "Don't."

"What? I can't help being grateful."

"I'm no hero." His voice was harsh and full of warning. "Far from it. I'm a selfish jerk."

"Y'all are wrong about that."

"No, I'm not." His eyes narrowed. "Would a knight in shining armor be this close to hitting on a woman who's injured?"

"Thinking is one thing. Doing is something else, and you didn't go there."

"Yet."

That's why he'd been so crabby; he'd been trying to distance himself.

He didn't need to tell her the attraction simmering between them could go the same way it had that night on his boat. The warning was always there. She didn't play fast and loose, and that was the only way he wanted to play. Both of them had equally compelling reasons to avoid anything intimate. So, here they were—between a rock and a hard place.

"I'll find somewhere else to stay."

"Damn it, Ellie—" He dragged his fingers through his hair and glared at her.

"What? We've already discussed this. I need this job and you don't sleep with anyone in Blackwater Lake. We slipped up once and got away with it but the second time could be a problem."

"Tell me something I don't know."

"I'll call M.J. at the Blackwater Lake Lodge."

"I thought you told me it was full," he said.

"It is, but she said if I couldn't find a place to call back and she'd help me."

He shook his head. "Not a good idea."

"Why not?"

"Then the word spreads around town that I tossed you into the street with a broken ankle. That would put a black mark on my reputation as much as—"

Sleeping with a woman and causing hard feelings that could cost him business. She knew that was what he'd been about to say. "Do you have a better solution? I'd love to hear it." She thought for a minute. "You've got family in town. Couldn't you stay with them?"

"For one thing, you'll need help until after my brother does the surgery on your ankle. And if I move out, it sends the wrong message."

"Which is?"

"That there's something going on between us. They'll make stuff up. That we can't be trusted to live under the same roof."

That was becoming the truth, she thought. "So you think it would cause more problems than it would solve?"

"Yes." He settled his hands on lean hips and shook his head, then met her gaze. "I don't think there's any choice. You have to stay here."

Ellie figured he knew this town pretty well and was probably right about this, so there was no alternative but to suck it up. Might as well put the most cheerful face on it. "We can do this. I'll just stay out of your way. After all, this is a pretty big house."

And he'd carried her through every square inch of it. Easily. As if she weighed nothing. Her heart wanted to sigh and swoon, but that was dangerous territory. She had her doubts that even the state of Montana would be big enough for them to avoid each other.

Chapter Six

Alex hadn't slept well with Ellie under his roof. Hair washing might have been heavenly for her, but it sent him to the seventh level of hell.

The feel of all the thick silky strands sliding through his fingers had haunted his dreams and never let him forget that she was right down the hall and would kiss him back if he went to her. He could live to be a hundred years old and would never understand what had possessed him to volunteer for this torture. It probably had something to do with the forlorn expression on her face at realizing nothing in her life was normal and wouldn't be for a while.

Of course, the situation being what it was, his life wouldn't be normal, either. And now he was working in his study until Ellie woke up and could determine whether or not she'd be coming with him to the job site.

"There's a strange woman in the guest room."

Martha Spooner, his housekeeper, stood in the doorway. She showed up every weekday morning at seven and usually went to work without saying hello because more often than not he'd already left the house. Obviously today she'd done that and happened on Ellie because he'd forgotten to intercept her and explain about his houseguest.

"Good morning to you, too," he said.

"It *was* good until I came across the strange woman in your guest room."

"She's from Texas and a little strange, I'll admit, but pretty harmless."

"She's pretty. The rest is unknown."

Martha was under five feet tall and so thin it was possible a good wind could carry her off. Barely sixty, she had short, curly salt-and-pepper hair and pale blue eyes that missed nothing. Her voice was deep and a little gravelly, a leftover from the smoking habit she'd kicked when she turned fifty and decided to get healthy for retirement. Personally, Alex thought she was still crabby from giving up nicotine, but Martha claimed it was an inherited trait from her mother's side. Bettencourts were notoriously crabby people, which could explain why this one never married or had children. His personal opinion was that she'd never retire, and selfishly he hoped to be proven right about that.

She walked farther into the study, stopping on the other side of his flattop oak desk covered with blueprints, renderings and construction elevations. Without saying a word, she stared at him, giving him her "bad cop" look designed to get information even out of a hardened criminal.

"What?" he finally asked.

"You know good and well," she said with a sternness that fooled no one into believing she wasn't soft as mush inside. "You never bring women home. I heard a rumor once about you being gay, and no female in Blackwater Lake could independently confirm that it was false. I'm pretty sure you like females but could be prejudiced because I work for you. The point is that you don't go out with anyone in town."

He grinned. "You noticed."

"Of course." Her dark brown eyes narrowed. "There are a lot of women around here who feel it's a man's duty to change their single status. When one slips through their fingers like you have, it draws attention."

Alex didn't plan to change his single status because to do that he'd have to get married. The first time had been an unqualified disaster, and nothing about it compelled him to repeat the experience. If he'd started down the dating road after moving back to town, he would have drawn attention for disappointing those single women. That caused hard feelings, and grudges were bad for business.

"I'm being diplomatic. You know why I don't get involved."

Martha's mouth pulled tight for a moment. "The former Mrs. McKnight."

"Laurel—"

"I wouldn't know. She insisted on being called *Mrs.*"

"Right."

Alex had talked to the ex about that and she'd insisted that employees shouldn't be on a first-name basis with the person signing the checks. "She's not Mrs. McKnight anymore."

She hadn't wasted any time becoming Mrs. Someone Else after leaving Alex. And she'd taken his boy with her. He would always think of that child as his, though he'd had no legal rights.

"So, you're stalling," Martha said. "Who's the lady and why is she here? Because Lord knows you're not involved with her."

He was doing his level best not to be. "How do you know that?"

"Hello." Her tone clearly said *duh.* "She's not in your bed. I can keep up this question-and-answer for a long time. And before you take that as a challenge, remember I'm on the clock. Your clock."

There were times, this being one of them, when Alex wished she wasn't the best housekeeper he'd ever had. He also wished he wasn't extremely fond of her because she presented certain challenges.

He sighed in surrender. "Her name is Ellie Hart and she's an architect."

"I heard about her. She's the one working on Mercy Medical Clinic with you."

"That's right."

Alex explained the situation, all except the part where the two of them had slept together once.

"So you're helping her out until she gets back on her feet." Martha nodded thoughtfully.

"That's all there is to it."

The housekeeper stared at him suspiciously. "If you go out of your way to say there's nothing else going on, it makes a person wonder what else is really going on."

This was not the best time to remember the advice of his divorce attorney, which was to give away as little as possible and know when to stop talking. A little information plus the fact that Martha Spooner knew him really well wasn't a good combination when trying to keep a situation off the small-town rumor radar.

"I can't stop you from wondering," he finally said.

"Got that right. I'm going to wonder the heck out of this, and so will the rest of the inquiring minds in Blackwater Lake."

"Martha—"

"What?" The expression on her face was as innocent as she could get it, what with that gleam in her eyes. "This is honest-to-goodness news."

"It's not a big deal."

She gave him a look that clearly stated, *If you have to say it's no big deal then it might, in fact,* be *a big deal.* "I have a duty—"

"To?"

"To share interesting tidbits that I come across. Such as how, out of the goodness of your heart, you're doing a nice thing for a stranger. Putting that poor woman with a broken ankle up because she can't climb stairs. That's a selfless act that people should know about."

And this was one of the challenges. "Look, Martha, is there anything I can say to persuade you to keep this quiet?"

She tapped her lip, thinking for a moment. "Nope."

A knock came from the open doorway, and Ellie stood there balancing on her crutches. "Hi. Hope I'm not interrupting."

"No." Only his being grilled like raw meat and he couldn't be sorry she'd stopped it. "Ellie Hart, this is my housekeeper, Martha Spooner."

Ellie hobbled closer, then balanced and held out her hand. "It's very nice to meet you."

"Same here, Miss Hart."

"Please call me Ellie."

"I will." Martha's eyebrow went up, and she gave him a look that said, *This one's an improvement but I'm still withholding judgment.*

"How's the ankle?" he asked.

"It doesn't hurt as much today. I'm ready to go to work." She looked down at the sweats she was still wearing. "Well, almost ready."

One look at her tousled, sun-streaked brown hair and fresh-faced prettiness and Alex was ready, too, but what popped into his mind had nothing to do with work. "It's okay to take the day off. After all you've been through a lot in the last twenty-four hours." He saw Martha's look and added, "With your ankle, I mean."

Ellie looked at him. "I'll cut the day short if necessary, but it's best to bank the time for later. Just in case."

"Whatever you say." He glanced at Martha and could almost see the wheels in her mind turning the words into something to put under the heading *News*.

"Okay, then. I'll go get ready." She used her friendly, dimpled smile on the housekeeper. "I'll do my very best not to be a bother to you. I promise y'all won't even know I'm here."

If only, Alex thought, but his luck wasn't that good. And it showed no signs of changing since Martha was practically quivering with excitement to share his situation. The two women left the room, and his housekeeper was promising coffee and breakfast.

He instantly abandoned any hope that the older woman would exercise discretion and keep this to herself. Shortly, the whole town would know that Ellie Hart was living with him. Some would accept the Good Samaritan explanation, but others not so much. There must be a way to head off the gossip.

He picked up the phone and called his sister.

After work Alex drove to his home from the job site, and Ellie sat beside him in the front seat of the truck.

"It was a long day," he said. "How do you feel?"

She noted the concern in his voice but the aviator sunglasses hid the expression in his eyes. She wouldn't blame him for being annoyed with the whole situation.

"My ankle doesn't hurt." Ellie glanced over at him. "That's not particularly surprising, since you wouldn't let me walk anywhere on my own except the bathroom."

"Just following doctor's orders," he said.

"Speaking of Ben, I updated him today. The cast is a little looser, and he said it means the swelling is going down. He wants me to stop by in a couple days to make sure, but he said the surgery will probably be a week from now."

"I'll drive you to the hospital," Alex offered.

"Before you officially volunteer, we should wait and see what's going on at the site. There's some delicate work ahead with meeting all the building codes for the dedicated X-ray and Magnetic Resonance Imaging rooms."

"You're right. But depending on where we are, if necessary we can schedule busywork for the crew for that day. Getting your ankle on the mend is the number one priority."

Ellie couldn't ever recall being a man's number one priority except the sleazeball married guy who'd made it his business to seduce her and ruin her life. What Alex just said started a lovely glow inside her. It wasn't wise to trust it, so she didn't.

"I'm as anxious to get back on my feet and return to my regularly scheduled life as you are to make it happen."

Alex glanced in the rearview mirror. "I think we're being followed."

"Really?" Ellie looked over her shoulder and saw a sporty little red compact behind them.

"It's my sister, Daisy Ray."

"Isn't her name Sydney?"

"That's what it says on her birth certificate, but she got the nickname about ten years ago. I was here for a visit and brought a buddy. We stopped in at the garage where she works with my dad, and she was wearing shapeless overalls covered with grease. Her hair was a mess. The guy said she smelled fresh as a daisy and looked like a ray of sunshine."

"How did she react?" Ellie hadn't met his sister yet but didn't want to make a bad impression.

"She liked the name and it stuck." Before there was time to evaluate the weird, mischievous smile he said, "Here we are. Home sweet home."

He pulled to a stop in front of the house and his sister parked behind them. "Sit tight and I'll help you out."

"That's okay. I can do it."

Ellie was starting to get the hang of the crutches and managed to get them out of the truck. Gravity was her friend when she slid out and propped herself up, but Alex wasn't too happy when he saw her.

"I told you to wait for me."

"It's time I manage for myself. These things are going to be around for a while."

"And Rome wasn't built in a day. Hurting yourself more will just set you back."

Sydney McKnight joined them and Ellie noticed the family resemblance, partly because she didn't look any happier than her brother. Ellie had brothers and knew from personal experience how judgmental sisters could be. Later she would think about why it was important to make a good impression, but right now the sister in question would be a tough nut to crack.

"Hi, Alex."

"Hey, Daisy Ray."

"Don't call me that." Sydney's brown eyes flashed with annoyance.

Ellie realized Alex had set her up and was glad she hadn't fallen into his trap and tried the nickname out.

Clearly it was a brother/sister thing. "He told me you liked to be called Daisy."

"My brother is a world-class toad." She gave him another glare for good measure then said, "Hi, I'm Sydney. I'd shake hands but it looks like yours are otherwise occupied."

"Yeah. Ellie Hart," she said, balancing on the crutches. "It's nice to meet you, Sydney."

When his sister pointedly didn't respond to that statement, Alex said, "To what do I owe the honor of a visit from my favorite sister?"

"I'm your only sister."

And she was gorgeous, in spite of the old jeans and shapeless white T-shirt with McKnight Automotive spelled out in big black letters on the front. She reminded Ellie of a young Catherine Zeta-Jones and was showing off some attitude that was all McKnight.

"Are you following me?" he teased.

"Are you going to invite me in?" she shot back.

"Of course." He slung his arm across her shoulders, then pulled her close and rubbed his knuckles across the top of her head.

"Hey, knock it off."

He looked back at Ellie. "Are you all right? I can carry you in."

"I'm fine." If you didn't count her inner conflict. Part of her wanted to be independent, but the other part sort of liked the way he took care of her. "I'll be along."

Watching the two of them made Ellie miss her own brothers. Lincoln called every day to check on her and had been ready to fly in from Dallas when he found out she'd broken her ankle. After convincing him she had things under control, he'd reminded her if she ever needed him, he would be there.

"Want a beer?" Alex's voice carried from the kitchen.

"Sure," his sister answered. "Got anything to go with that?"

"I think so."

Ellie click-clacked into the room as he was pulling cheese out of the refrigerator. "Let me slice that."

Alex gave her a disapproving look. "Go sit in the family room. And elevate that foot."

"But—"

"Daisy can help me." He pointed at her. "Don't argue. Doctor's orders, remember?"

"Wow, you're really bossy."

"If I were you, Ellie," his sister said, "I'd tell him where to go."

"I would, if he were wrong. But your other brother did tell me to stay off my feet as much as possible so the swelling would go down. And I think it's working."

"Okay, then. Go put it up," he ordered.

Ellie hobbled out of the room but heard Sydney ask, "You don't need any help in here, do you?" There was a mumbled reply to which she answered, "Okay. I'll keep your friend company."

Ellie was touched by the words until noting the emphasis on the words "your friend" where the tone reeked of hostility and distrust. The truth was if one of her brothers was in a similar situation, she'd have had the same reaction. Sydney was here to see what was going on and run interference if necessary.

When she settled on the leather couch in front of the flat-screen TV with her foot on a throw pillow, Sydney sat in front of her on the large leather ottoman that doubled as a coffee table.

It was best to deal with this in a straightforward way. "You're here to defend your brother's honor."

The other woman looked surprised. "Do I need to?"

"As you can probably see, I broke my ankle."

"So Alex told me." That sounded a lot as if she didn't want to accept as true the evidence in front of her.

But Ellie zeroed in on something else. "You talked to him?"

"He called me first thing this morning, and I wanted to see for myself what's going on here."

"Nothing." That was the honest truth at this moment in time. There was no good reason to bring up anything that had transpired previously. "The apartment I rented is upstairs, and with the cast it's impossible for me to get up and down. The lodge is completely full, so that wasn't an option. Alex very kindly offered to help me out."

"He told me that, too."

"You don't believe him?" Ellie didn't see that she was making any headway on the trust front even with the cast and crutches to prove it.

"It's not him I don't believe."

"So you think I'm using him."

"It's happened before." Syd's eyes brimmed with suspicion and sparkled with dislike.

"He told me about his wife."

"So you can see where I'm coming from." The other woman leaned forward. "The thing is, my mother died giving birth to me. My dad was in shock and grieving. He had a business to run and no emotional reserves. Friends and neighbors helped out some when I was a baby, but Alex was the one who stepped in to raise Ben and me. He did it until we were big enough to be on our own. Ben went to college and I hung out at the garage with my dad while going to college. Alex took off for California because it was way past time for him to have a turn at footloose and fancy-free."

"That's a lot of responsibility."

"No kidding. And that witch took advantage of him." There was determination in Sydney's eyes. "Now he needs me to look after him."

"If you ask me, he's big enough to take care of himself. Just saying…."

Before the other woman could retort, the man in question walked into the room. "Beer for you, Daisy."

"Don't call me that." She grabbed the longneck bottle from him.

He looked at Ellie. "White wine?"

"Sounds good." Boy, could she use it.

He handed over the glass, then crossed his arms over his chest. "So, what are you ladies talking about?"

"Ellie was telling me how you invited her to stay here." Sydney took a sip from her beer.

"Yeah." He sat on the couch, far enough to keep from bumping the injured ankle. "It's just business."

"Really?" His sister's tone said she didn't believe that any more than if he'd told her elephants could fly.

"It's true. There's no time to find another architect, and I can't afford to have her out of commission. She needed a place without stairs to stay, and I've got plenty of room. It's as simple as that."

"There's nothing simple about inviting a total stranger into your home."

"Ellie's not a total stranger." He met her gaze and smiled a smile that said he was thinking about that night on his boat. "We're friends, too. All I'm doing is helping her out."

"Just a roof over her head."

"That and I'm driving her to the hospital when she has the surgery."

"What surgery?"

Ellie knew he wouldn't violate her medical privacy, so

she answered. "Repairing the broken bone will require a procedure to put in a plate to hold it together so the healing can happen properly. Your brother Ben is doing it."

"I figured."

"So, while I appreciate the attack-dog routine, it's really not necessary." Alex stood and kissed the top of her head. "You can stand down, Daisy."

"If you don't stop calling me that—"

"What?" he said.

"Give me time. I'll think of something."

"Yeah, yeah. You're meddling," he said. "I can return the favor. Why are you taking a break from men?"

"Ben has a big mouth."

"So you don't want to talk about it?" Alex guessed.

"About as much as I'd want to skydive out of a perfectly good airplane."

"Okay, then. My work here is done, and I'm going to get food now." He walked back to the kitchen and out of earshot again.

The soft expression on Sydney's face disappeared, replaced by a fierce, protective look. "He's a really good guy."

"You'll get no argument from me."

"Okay, then. There's nothing more I can say to him."

"I have brothers, too. Believe me, I understand how you're feeling about this."

"I'm not finished yet." The other woman drilled her with a look. "Consider yourself warned. If you hurt him, there's nowhere you can hide that I won't find you."

"Sydney, he's not looking for emotional attachments and neither am I." Maybe if she told just a little of her past it would strengthen her case. "A couple years ago I had a really bad relationship."

"Join the club. I'm taking a hiatus from men."

"So you can understand what's going on here," Ellie said.

"Not when it's my brother."

"Okay. Then you'll just have to take my word that this situation is just temporary. I like Alex and would never do anything to hurt him."

She stopped talking. There were no words to convince his sister that she wasn't weaving some elaborate scheme to do Alex harm. But what if *he* hurt *her?* Ellie thought. It could happen. There was an attraction and they were stuck with the circumstances. Syd was right, but not the way she thought.

There was nowhere to hide, either from Alex or from the feelings for him that seemed to grow stronger every day that Ellie was stuck under his roof.

Chapter Seven

"I'm fine, Lincoln. Dr. McKnight said the surgery went as expected. In four weeks the cast will come off and my ankle will be good as new." Ellie shifted her weight on Alex's family room sofa to get more comfortable, then adjusted the cell phone to her ear.

"Way to go, baby sister. So you're better, faster, stronger? Like the bionic woman?"

"This is real life," she answered.

"Yeah, and you don't sound fine."

"How do I sound?"

"Drunk or hungover. I can't decide which."

"I'm just tired. The procedure was scheduled for early this morning, and the closest hospital is about seventy-five miles away."

"That's crazy." Lincoln Hart sounded truly shocked and it took a lot to shock her seen-it-all, done-it-all brother. "What the hell are you doing in— Where are you? Black Hole, Montana?"

"It's Blackwater Lake. A wonderful, warm place." *Don't make fun of it,* she wanted to add. "And you know good and well why I'm here."

"The medical clinic."

"Right. I did the design and drew up the plans. Now from firsthand experience I see why there's a need for an outpatient surgery center. When it's open, patients won't have to go almost a hundred miles away for the procedure I just had."

"Now that I think about it… Please tell me you didn't drive yourself to the hospital," Linc said sharply.

"Of course not."

"Don't of-course-not me, Miss I-can-do-it-myself. Remember who you're talking to. I know you better than anyone."

"That's true."

He was six years older, but still closer to her in age than Cal and Sam. Katherine and Hastings Hart had three boys one after the other and only a year apart. They'd thought the family was complete until Ellie. She was an oops or a surprise, neither of which was a good thing, at best an afterthought.

Lincoln was her rock. He'd held her while she'd cried after the humiliation of being "the other woman" and her subsequent termination from the job. He'd sympathized for a week, then said it was time to be over it. Her brother routinely got over a relationship in under twenty-four hours so, in his opinion, seven days had been a luxury. But Ellie was convinced that no woman had ever really captured his heart, and that was why he threw them away like used tissues.

"Are you listening to me?" he said.

She started to say *of course,* then caught herself. He did know her pretty well. "Sorry."

"Are you in pain?"

"Not much." She was a little surprised by that, but the doctor had said the injury probably hurt more before being set. "It aches a little, but nothing an over-the-counter pain killer can't handle."

"Where are you now?"

"On the sofa with my foot elevated."

Alex had carried her from the truck as if she weighed nothing and settled her in his family room, but those were details she kept to herself. She'd never told Linc about her upstairs apartment and the change in living arrangement after her accident. Some things a protective brother was better off not knowing about his sister. And she was pretty sure if she told, it would be impossible not to reveal that her feelings for this particular coworker were more than they should be.

"Is someone there with you?"

"Yes. A friend from work."

"Tell her she better take good care of you or she'll have to answer to me. It's my duty as your big brother."

"I'll do that."

"You're sure I don't need to come to Black Hole and take care of you?"

"Absolutely not." Ellie knew he loved her and meant well, but an obligation was something she didn't want to be.

"Okay, El. I have to go. Got a meeting. Big deal in the works. There could be an assignment in it for my favorite architect."

"Y'all have to say that because I'm your sister." Alex walked into the room with a mug of tea that looked small in his big hand. Her heart did that shimmy-shake thing that always made her breath catch when she saw him.

Apparently Linc noticed. "I heard that. You sure you're okay?"

"Fine. Really. I'll talk to you soon, Linc. Say hi to everyone for me. Love you."

"Back at you. Bye, sis."

She ended the call and set her cell phone on the sofa table next to the couch. After taking the steaming mug from Alex she said, "Thanks. Just what the doctor ordered."

"Actually he ordered you to rest and keep the ankle elevated as much as possible."

She glanced at her new hot-pink, below-the-knee cast carefully resting on pillows. Her toenails were almost the same shade and the polish was chipped. When her leg was liberated, the first thing she'd do was a pedicure. The second thing would be buying new sweatpants. This pair and the two others had only one-and-a-half legs since Alex had done a surprisingly neat job of cutting off the left ones.

"I'll do my best to be your brother's star patient. If I succeed, it will be thanks to you."

He sat down on the leather ottoman and rested his elbows on his knees. "It's time to eat something. You've been fasting since last night."

"I'm not very hungry."

"Tell it to someone who's not responsible for getting you back on your feet."

Wow, she was on a roll. The second man in less than five minutes who reminded her that she was a duty. So much for Miss I-can-do-it-myself.

"I'll get my appetite back if I can just rest for a while."

"Sometimes choking down a little food, whether you want it or not, will help things along."

"The thought of it turns my stomach."

"How about a little chicken noodle soup and ginger ale?"

"You're not going to let this go until I do, are you?"

He shook his head. There was an expression in his dark eyes that was all about determination. "What do you say?"

"I don't have the energy to argue."

"Okay, then. Coming right up." He stood and it seemed as if he couldn't get out of the room fast enough.

Ellie couldn't blame him, what with her being such a burden and all. She set the mug on the table beside her cell phone, then rested her cheek against the sofa back and her eyes drifted closed. It wasn't food that turned her stomach so much as knowing that Alex must be counting the days until he could wash his hands of her.

She absolutely hated having to depend on someone, especially a man who didn't want her there. His reasons were practical. In her case, getting her career back was the path to self-reliance, self-support and no more family jokes about being the only one who'd taken a detour on the road to success. She just wanted them to be as proud of her as she was of the rest of the Harts. So she had to grit her teeth and get through this as best she could.

The smell of food made her eyes pop open, and her stomach growled.

"I heard that." Alex was holding a tray with a steaming bowl of something and a glass.

"I must have zoned out." She sat up straighter and settled her injured leg more securely on the pillows.

"Good for you." Alex set the tray on her thighs, then sat down beside her. "Now eat."

"Yes, sir."

She dipped the soup spoon into the hot broth and scooped up noodles, chicken chunks and vegetables. After blowing on it, she ate. Then she repeated the process until the bowl was empty. "That was really good. I didn't know you could cook."

"Can't, but I'm an expert reheater. You can thank Martha."

"I will."

She picked up the glass with ice and bubbly liquid the color of weak apple juice. The sweet, cold, sparkling drink went down easily, and she felt much stronger. Apparently she'd needed to eat.

As she sipped, she glanced around the room. She'd spent some time in this spot since Alex had brought her here a week or so ago. Somehow she hadn't paid much attention to the details, but things jumped out at her now. The carpet was beige and the entertainment center featuring the flat-screen TV would be the envy of any guy.

Framed black-and-white enlarged snapshots of the local mountains and lake hung on the walls. Behind the couch was an oak sofa table with a brass lamp topped by a cream-colored shade, and framed photographs were displayed on either side. There was one of a baby boy who must be the child Alex had once believed was his. Others were of his family with an older man she'd never met. But she recognized Ben and Sydney.

They were all grown up now, and she remembered what his sister had said. Alex had done his best to fill the empty place left by his mother's death. Then he'd taken off for California because it was way past having his turn at footloose and fancy-free.

"What are you thinking?" he asked. "Before you say nothing, you should know that I can see the wheels turning."

"I was just wondering how old you were when you left home."

"Nineteen."

Ellie had been just a year younger when she'd gone to college in Texas—the University of Dallas, which wasn't far from home. She'd had her safety net close by and still was nervous about leaving it.

"Were you scared?"

He shook his head. "I couldn't get out of here fast enough."

"Why?" Ellie wanted to hear it from him.

"I was tired of being the oldest, expected to look after the other two. It was time to do my own thing, make my own mistakes and not have to worry about the ones all three of us were making." He met her gaze. "I guess that makes me a selfish jerk, but it's the truth."

"Honesty is always the best policy."

"I just wanted to go somewhere people didn't look at me with pity in their eyes because I was that poor boy who'd lost his mother and had to look after his younger brother and sister."

So Sydney wasn't exaggerating. Alex had felt leaving the state of Montana was necessary to escape the responsibility he'd assumed at such a young age. He'd supported himself, attended college and started a business. Then he'd fallen in love and assumed responsibility again when the woman he fell in love with announced she was pregnant. That sure bit him in the backside.

But even though he'd run from responsibility, he'd brought Ellie here to his home and took care of her, carrying her to prevent more injury to her leg. Not all of that was because of the job they were doing at the clinic. At heart, this man was a caretaker whether he wanted to admit it or not. Her realization was both comforting and unsettling.

He was a great guy, not the kind who would seduce her, lie about being married then throw her under the bus.

He was so honest that he'd told her up front that he would never trust again and wasn't the marrying kind. She wasn't looking to get serious, either, but every time she saw him or touched him, he made her want.

She glanced at the photos again. "In spite of wanting so badly to get away, you came back. Are you sorry, Alex? I mean other than what happened after you got here."

"It's a good place to live. Fresh air. Beautiful scenery. Lots of work. Nice people."

She remembered him telling her he'd come back because it was a great place to raise kids. He didn't say that now when listing the town attributes, because he only played fast and loose. That meant he wouldn't settle down and have a family, which made her sad for him, sad that he wouldn't take a chance on giving his heart again.

She turned her head and caught him looking at her with a hungry expression that turned his dark eyes black. Her insides responded and turned to liquid fire, making her hot all over. It was also a revelation. He pretended disinterest, but she was pretty sure he was fighting the attraction simmering between them as hard as she was. If only she could rewind and delete what had happened on his boat.

If she hadn't experienced one night of heaven in his arms, resisting him now wouldn't be hell on earth.

"I don't know about this," Alex said.

They'd come home from work together and were in the kitchen getting ready to make dinner. This was a great kitchen with rich, elegant black-and-beige swirls running through granite countertops. The appliances and sink were stainless steel. A cooktop, with microwave above and double ovens to the left, rounded out the cool culinary toys. Ellie was dying to do something domestic in here and he was trying to get in her way.

He'd told her to sit down at one of the bar stools on the other side of the island, but she wasn't in the mood to be as useless as a plastic plant. She was jumpy and her skin felt too tight.

So Ellie stood her ground in front of the cooktop and put on the stubborn face that never failed to convince her brothers she meant business. "We can do this the easy way or the hard way. I've been sitting around so long now, I'm getting a muffin top."

"Ellie—" He stopped and blinked at her. "A what?"

"It's the roll of flab just above your waistband and happens when pants get too tight because a person isn't allowed to move around as much as she used to."

"I don't see any muffin top."

He was checking her out from the top of her head down to the denim shorts and snug white T-shirt hugging her torso and hips. There was heat in his eyes before he banked it, and that was empowering, unsettling and dangerous. She needed to do something, keep her hands occupied before this turned into trouble.

"Be that as it may," she said in response to his muffin-top comment, "I want to help. I can help and I'm going to."

"How do you propose to do that?"

He folded his arms over his chest and leaned back against the oak cabinet. Two could play the "looking someone over" game, and she gave as good as she got. No muffin top or beer belly on him. His shoulders were wide and tapered to a chest with contours and muscles she remembered far too well. Narrow hips and long legs made her heart beat even harder than it did from the exertion of moving around on crutches.

It was a little safer to look at his face, so that was what she did. "You said Martha did the marketing and stocked the fridge. There's eggs, bread, vegetables and fruit, no?"

"That's right. And your point?"

"Omelets." At the blank look she added, "You be the gopher. I'll stand in one spot and cut stuff up. Then I'll park myself in front of the pan and cook it. Everything else is up to you."

"I don't know about this," he said again. "Are you sure the pain is gone?"

It was incredibly sweet of him to worry, but she stopped short of letting herself believe the concern was anything more than an intense commitment to getting her better and out of his house. That was safer than going into a starry-eyed slide that would end in a very hard landing.

"Alex—" She balanced the crutches under her arms and touched his wide wrist, just for a moment letting herself savor the warmth of his skin. "You'd know if I was lying when I told you the pain is gone. It is, and now there's nothing left but deep annoyance."

"About?"

"My leg is starting to itch, which I'm determined to believe is from the healing process. These darn crutches are awkward, and getting around takes me longer and I hate that. The only thing that hurts is being forced to change my routine, but I'm coming to terms with that. By the time I have a new normal in place, the cast will be off. In the meantime, I can do everything I did before. All it requires are adjustments."

He looked down. "I still can't believe you let those knuckleheads on the construction crew sign your cast."

Ellie shivered, remembering the intensity in Alex's eyes when a few of the guys squatted down by her leg, big callused hands wielding a Sharpie instead of a power drill. It was all in good fun, but you wouldn't know it by the look on their boss's face. She was tempted to believe he'd been jealous but was too smart to go there.

"How could I say no? That had the potential for hard feelings, and unhappiness in the ranks doesn't promote harmony in the workplace." She shrugged. "You're taking one for the team by letting me stay with you. The fact they wanted to sign the cast made me feel included in the crew. Doesn't seem smart to do anything that would disrupt the positive work flow we've got going. It's the best way to reach the goal line."

"I see your point. But for the next month you'll be walking around with 'Live fast, love hard and don't break anything else' on the front of your leg."

"Yeah." She laughed ruefully, looking down at the big bold words running across the pink material covering her shin. "At least it's not a tattoo."

"True. That would be above and beyond the call of duty." He grinned. "It's permanent."

And neither of them wanted that.

She took one last lingering look at the way his T-shirt tightened around the smooth, tempting muscle of his upper arm, then forced herself to think about cooking.

"Okay, get out the carton of eggs, mushrooms, green onions. Is there any cheese?"

Alex opened the refrigerator and looked. "Yeah. Chunks of Swiss and cheddar."

"Swiss. Do you have a grater?"

He slid her a wry look. "This might be a bachelor pad, but it's not the wilderness."

"So you're saying Martha stocked all the necessary kitchen gizmos to have what she needs for cooking?"

He lifted one broad shoulder. "She got tired of not having the right tool for a job, so I gave her the go-ahead to make this kitchen her own."

"Reading between the lines, I'm going to guess that you don't have a clue where she puts anything."

"That's harsh."

"But accurate since you didn't deny it."

"Think of it like the keyboard on a computer—hunt and peck for what you need."

"All I want is a cheese grater. Or a food processor will do."

He rummaged through drawers and cupboards, which took some time because there were so many. "Apparently I have several choices. Flat. One that stands up like an oil rig. And, last but not least, an appliance that could grind tree trunks into wood chips."

"Flat is fine. No point in pulverizing the poor cheese. It will melt, anyway."

At Ellie's direction, Alex fetched, carried and assembled vegetables to be sliced and the tools to do it with. It seemed as if the more she tried to stay out of his way, the more she was right where he was going. Every time it happened the expression on his face turned just a little darker and more disapproving.

She tried to ignore it and threw herself into the task at hand, leaning against the island counter while preparing the fresh ingredients. He kept out of her way, setting the table and finding the four-slice toaster from one of the upper cabinets. When the omelet components were ready, she propped herself on the crutches and swung herself to the cooktop, where she stir-fried the veggies. Then she cracked eggs into a bowl, added milk and whipped the mixture with a wire whisk.

She poured it into a preheated pan and at the right time put in the vegetables and cheese, then folded the egg mixture over.

"Time to toast," she announced.

"Got it covered."

He brought two plates with buttered toast over to her

and watched while she divided the omelet in half and slid some onto each dish.

"Dinner is served."

"Looks good. Now go sit down," he ordered.

This time she did as he said and waited until Alex set the food in front of her. He took the chair directly across the round oak table. After eating a bite, he said, "Good."

She tasted her own eggs and nodded appreciatively. "I like it, too."

That wasn't all she liked. The view was pretty amazing and an entirely new experience. In the middle of her affair with the jerk, she hadn't noticed that he always met her after dinner, then was gone, never taking her out in public or spending the night. She'd always wanted to make him a meal but it never worked out. What a dope she'd been.

Part of her was glad that the creep hadn't tainted the experience of cooking for a man, and she was glad Alex was her first. The other part warned not to get too used to this.

"I saw you showing your brother around the clinic addition," she said.

Alex nodded. "It's all framed, and before we put up wallboard now's the time to make any changes."

"I'm sorry I couldn't do the walk with you." They'd agreed that with her on crutches it would be tricky to negotiate the tour.

"As it turns out," he said, looking up from his plate, "you did such a good job on the blueprints, the three-dimensional computer rendering and walking the doctors through everything, they're getting exactly what was expected. Got a thumbs-up from both Ben and Adam."

"That's great news."

She waited for him to pick up the conversation, but he didn't. The rest of the meal was completed in silence.

When they'd finished eating, he said, "You cooked, I'll do the dishes."

"I can help."

"But you don't have to. Why don't you go relax and watch TV?"

"It seems wrong to leave you in here alone."

"I'm used to it."

Right. Duh. Because he never brought women here.

Alex cleared the table and she followed him over to the sink, trying to figure out what she could do to help. After rinsing off a plate, he held it and looked at her.

She glanced down at the dishwasher and got it. "Sorry. I'm underfoot." She backed up, which took a lot more time and coordination than moving forward.

"Really, Ellie, go in the family room and put your feet up."

"Okay, if you're sure."

"Very." There was an edge to his voice.

She maneuvered around the dishwasher door and Alex moved at the same time. She was in his way again.

"Sorry."

She was attempting to go sideways, the movement anything but graceful. She started to lose her balance but would have caught herself. Except she didn't have to.

Alex put his hands at her waist to steady her. He tightened his grip and started to lift her, get her out of his way, but that's not what happened.

He stared at her mouth for several moments and seemed to be fighting some internal battle, a conflict only he understood. Then he swore softly, lowered his head and touched his lips to hers.

Chapter Eight

Ellie opened her mouth and Alex slid his tongue inside. When he stroked and caressed the moist interior, fire raced through all her girlie parts. Losing herself in the moment, she put her arms around his neck and her crutches fell sideways, but he held her tight, drawing her close to his body. She could feel that he wanted her as much as she wanted him.

So nothing had changed since the first time. It hadn't been a fluke, and that was more important to her than she'd realized.

Happiness poured through her, and she didn't think she could fight the feeling even if she wanted to. As if he could read her mind, Alex swept her up into his arms, and she rested her head on his shoulder, savoring the easy strength as he carried her down the hall. Moments later they were in his bedroom, and he set her down on the bench at the foot of the bed. She watched as he turned down the comforter.

"This is the first time I've been in your room." That first night, he'd carried her past and pointed it out, but they hadn't gone inside. Since then, she'd felt it was a violation of privacy and wouldn't be anything more than snooping because they didn't have an intimate relationship. She was about to be proven wrong about that.

"What do you think of the place?" His voice was husky, impatient.

"The place" was masculine, with dresser and night-stands in dark wood. The comforter was a geometric pattern of black and beige. The floor was wood, a stain that complemented the furniture. The space suited Alex.

"It's very you."

He met her gaze. "Is that good or bad?"

"I'll let you know."

When he finished with the bedding and the sheets were exposed, he came back to her. The sun was going down and shadows crawled into the room, but she could see the intensity in his eyes, and it set her on fire.

He knelt down in front of her and their eyes met. "Do you want to leave?"

"No." The word was just a whisper.

He smiled then leaned forward and kissed her. She really liked the touch of his mouth against the corner of hers, the way he touched the side of her nose and trailed nibbling kisses across her cheek and down her neck to... Oh, my, she loved it when he found that spot just beneath her ear that drove her insane.

"Alex—" Her head fell back, exposing her neck to his attention to detail. He was panting, his breath fractured, and hers was an echo of it.

"I want to undress you."

Every word penetrated her skin and turned her blood to liquid fire. "What's stopping you?"

"For one thing, you're sitting."

"Yeah. Sorry. I dropped the crutches." She rubbed her thumb across the pounding pulse point in his neck. "As an architect, I've learned that every problem has a fix."

"Oh?" His mouth quirked up in a lopsided grin. "And what's your solution, hotshot?"

"Just put me where you want me." Ellie watched the fire in his eyes burn hotter.

He smiled, then stood and lifted her in his arms before settling her on the bed. Then he put one knee down and moved toward her like a predator. He straightened over her and grabbed the hem of his T-shirt, yanking it over his head before tossing it into one of the shadows darkening the floor. Seconds later he reached over and pulled off her shirt, launching it somewhere in the vicinity of his.

Ellie held her breath as he stretched out a hand to get to her bra closure. With a flick of his fingers he released it then dragged the straps down her arms. Heat flashed in his eyes as he looked at her. As if unable to resist, he slowly reached out and with his index finger, traced a circle around the peak of her left breast.

"Perfect," he breathed.

"I know what you mean," she said, brushing her finger over the contours of his chest.

Then he was backing off the bed, and disappointment clutched its way through her. "Where are you going?"

"Not far."

He opened a drawer in the nightstand and pulled out a square foil packet. Condom. Later she would think about the fact that he didn't bring women here but had them, anyway. About whether he kept them for the occasional female guest or it was a recent precaution because of her. The sight of him releasing his belt and dragging off jeans and boxers drove every other thought from her mind. His skin was bronze and his muscles rippled. He was all man and for this moment in time he was all hers.

She held out her arms and he instantly came back to her, folding her against him. They were chest to chest, skin to skin and her senses hummed with the pleasure of it. Vaguely she was aware of him sliding his thumb inside the waistband of her shorts. Gotta love elastic. But she lay back on the mattress and lifted her hips, helping to speed this up. She couldn't ever remember wanting something as much as she wanted him right now.

In seconds she was as naked as he and felt him cup her right breast, holding the peak as he lowered his head and took the straining tip into his mouth. She closed her eyes as he tugged gently, repeatedly filling her with pleasure-fueled tension. Squirming, her body took over, hips instinctively straining to let him know what she wanted.

"Alex—"

Just his name spoken in that needy tone told him everything. He rolled away, and she heard the efficient rip of the packet he'd set beside them. In the next instant, he settled his body over hers, his leg scraping the cast. The touch made him freeze, as if he'd just remembered.

"Oh, God, Ellie— Did I hurt you?"

"No. I'm fine. Don't stop." She settled her hands on the warm skin at his waist, urging him to keep going.

Very carefully he lowered his body over hers. She rested her palm on his chest, letting the dusting of hair tickle her fingers while she felt the thump of his wildly beating heart. Then they were skin to skin again as he slowly filled her and took her mouth at the same time.

It was as if they were the only two people in the universe. All the problems, the conflicts, were outside this bed where he was making love to her.

He pulled his mouth away and lifted slightly, relieving

her of some of his weight as he began to rock against her. The friction brushed and caressed her nerve endings and built the tension until there was no holding back. All the while she'd been fighting this, pressure had built up inside her just waiting to be released. Now pleasure poured through her in a soul-shattering liberation and he held her gently, cupping the back of her head in his palm.

When her tremors subsided, he pressed deeper inside her, lengthening the thrusts until he shuddered. He pressed her to him as he found his release, and it felt as if he'd never let her go. Time seemed to stop as they lay in each other's arms, then finally Alex stirred and softly kissed her.

"I'll be right back." He pulled the sheet up over her naked body, the same protective gesture as the last time.

She nodded and her eyes drifted closed, but somewhere close by she knew when a light went on, then off again. There was just enough time to wonder if this would be like the last encounter on his boat, when she'd dressed in a hurry and left. Except she was sort of stuck in his bed, because her crutches were on the floor in the kitchen. Before she could come up with a fix to the problem, he slid in and nestled her to his side.

What the heck, she thought, then relaxed and rested her cheek on his chest. This was different. Neither of them said anything for a few moments, then both spoke at once.

"I didn't mean for that to happen—"

"What am I going to do with you?" He sighed, then said, "Normally it's ladies first with me, but I've got something to get off my chest."

She thought about drawing his attention to the fact that she was on his chest, but figured that wasn't what he meant. "Okay. You first."

"It has to be acknowledged that our verbal agreement not to sleep together is a complete and utter failure."

"I noticed," she said. "Normally I'm a much higher achiever than this."

"I know what you mean. But it can be explained."

"Oh?"

He rubbed his chin over her hair. "There's no point in denying that I'm attracted to you."

Ellie wasn't sure whether or not that was a good thing, but it was definitely mutual. And this confirmed what she'd suspected, that he'd been fighting it just as she had. It would explain condoms at the ready when he normally took himself on a long weekend out of town to scratch that itch.

"And I guess the fact that I'm in your bed makes it pointless to deny that I find you just the tiniest bit attractive, too." Being draped over his chest, she felt the vibration of his laughter. "So, in deference to the agreement we made, I'll move back to my apartment."

"It's still upstairs," he pointed out.

"I'm on the mend. I'll just hop. Or crawl."

He thought about that. "You're Texas tough and could probably do that, but not if you had to carry anything. Like food, for instance. Or any other supplies required to live on your own. Hair product alone would require a crane."

"Very funny." But she could see what he meant. "Maybe I could have stuff delivered?"

"Even if that kind of service was available in a town as small as Blackwater Lake, I don't think it's wise, logistically speaking, to go that route. What with a little less than a month left in the cast, it's not worth the risk of doing further damage. That could delay the medical clinic expansion and, as previously established, neither of us wants that," he added.

Again she got his drift. "Then we'll just have to try harder so this doesn't happen again—"

"I've got another idea."

"Okay. Let's hear it." She couldn't imagine any other alternative, but was open to possibilities.

He brushed his thumb over her upper arm raising tingles that went to her toes. "We already broke our word once. To avoid the guilt of doing it again, and the negative self-esteem issues generated by another failure, I propose that we just have a fling instead."

"What?" She couldn't believe she'd heard right. It was a good thing Ellie wasn't on her feet. The shock of those words would have landed her on her backside. "Alex, you know as well as I do why we agreed sex wouldn't work—"

"I thought we did it just fine."

"You know that's not what I meant."

"Just hear me out." He was quiet for a moment and she was speechless so the silence stretched between them. "The thing is, you have your concerns and I have mine. But we also like each other. Right?"

"Yes," she conceded. But he was advocating making it more and that was probably stupid.

"So we give in and get this out of our systems. Have fun. No strings attached. No one gets hurt. When Mercy Medical Clinic comes to a successful conclusion, so will we."

"Because I'm leaving town." She knew that meant he didn't have to leave to get what he wanted the way he usually did. And she liked that there wouldn't be anyone else for him during that time.

"Right."

"We both go back to our regularly scheduled lives." She was thinking out loud.

"See? We're already thinking the same way."

"Let me see if I have this right." She was kind of glad that in this position, she didn't have to look at him. "Y'all are suggesting a physical relationship based on friendship and pleasure without emotional entanglements. In other words, I should act like a man."

"Well, you've got the basic idea, but I'd prefer you act like yourself."

That made her smile. One of the things she liked best about him was his ability to do that.

Ellie thought over what he'd proposed. Resisting Alex hadn't worked very well, and putting her heart all the way into the last relationship had been a disaster. It was easier and more convenient to stay here with him except for the pesky attraction going on. Since she was going back to Texas when the job ended, there didn't seem to be a lot to lose. By definition, flings had a short shelf life.

"I like your room, Alex." She snuggled closer. "Count me in."

Alex slapped his cell phone closed and resisted the urge to throw it across the construction trailer. The supplier had asked for an extra two days and he was acting as if it was two years. Having great sex with Ellie the past three nights should have made him a whole lot more relaxed than he was. Watching her through the trailer window from his desk inside, he was trying to figure out why he wanted to put his fist through a wall.

Maybe it would help him find some peace in breaking his own rule. He was having fun, all right, and enjoying the hell out of Ellie Hart in his bed until the next day at work when he couldn't take his eyes off her. It was a bad time to notice that having a fling with her came with complications.

Before he took that thought further, he spotted his

brother the doctor headed this way. In the white lab coat and green scrubs he stood out from the construction crew like a fly in milk.

Then the trailer door opened and Ben McKnight walked inside. "Hi, big brother."

Grateful for the distraction, Alex stood and walked around his desk to shake hands. "Hey. To what do I owe the honor of a visit from Blackwater Lake's best orthopedic specialist?"

"I'd be flattered if I wasn't the *only* specialist in town. I just came over to see you because I could."

Funny, Alex thought. He'd been working on Mercy Medical clinic for a while, and the only times he'd seen his brother were when Ellie broke her ankle and at the tour to update him on the progress of the project.

"I wasn't looking forward to the construction process, but it hasn't interfered with seeing patients at the clinic. It's going better than I expected," Ben said.

Alex knew people thought the two McKnight brothers could be twins, but he didn't see it. They were both a little over six feet tall with brown eyes and dark hair, but Ben had their father's nose and mouth. Alex's features favored his mother. Before she died, she'd taken care of everyone, and he'd easily stepped into the role when she was gone. Going to California had been a rebellion, an attempt to shake off the responsibility. But the way he'd stepped up with Ellie was making him wonder if the tendency wasn't hardwired into his DNA.

"Alex?"

The expression on Ben's face made it clear he was waiting for a response to a question, but Alex had no idea what he'd said. He didn't usually zone out, and it was particularly annoying in front of his brother.

"Sorry. Got a lot on my mind. What did you say?"

"The clinic expansion looks like it's coming along really well."

They'd been through this when he updated both of the clinic doctors. "We're a little ahead of schedule."

That's what made his reaction to an insignificant delay in a relatively minor list of supplies so surprising.

"Great." Ben rested his hands on lean hips. His stethoscope was draped around his neck. "Isn't that unusual?"

"Stuff always happens and you try to pad the time frame a little for the client just in case. But there are also factors that can work in your favor."

"Such as?"

"Working with a good architect."

Alex recalled his brother calling Ellie a belle from the Lone Star state, all big hair, sexy Southern drawl and attitude. Except for the big hair, he'd been right on.

"I saw Ellie talking to the construction crew on my way over here just now."

Alex glanced out the window and had no trouble finding her, thanks to that hot-pink cast. "She's out there every day, charming every last ounce of work out of those guys, and they don't even realize they're being maneuvered. Shooting the breeze with them, remembering names and their kids' names. Pep talks. I'll bet she was a high school cheerleader."

"Impressive." There was a definite spark of interest in Ben's eyes.

"And she does it all while hobbling around on those darn crutches. That doesn't even slow her down anymore."

"She's quite a woman," his brother agreed.

Alex felt his stomach knot up and knew exactly what had caused it. Jealousy. He recognized the feeling even after all this time. It's the way he'd reacted when his wife had announced she was leaving him for the father of her baby. Anger had consumed him later, and he was pretty sure he'd hit all the stages of grief before reaching his current philosophy of not getting emotionally involved. It was safer that way.

The thing was, he realized that Ben was trying to get a rise out of him for some reason. No way his brother would hit on Ellie since he was already in love with and engaged to another woman. Alex was determined not to give him any reaction.

"So, how's that fiancée of yours?" he asked.

"Camille is fine. Working hard at the lodge."

"Have you two set a wedding date yet?"

"Still trying to narrow that down. We want to be settled in the house first."

Alex had been the contractor, and he knew every square inch of his brother's house because he'd personally supervised and inspected the work. "The painters are scheduled and finishing touches are all that's left."

"Cam hired a decorator and they're picking out colors, coordinating furniture and window coverings." Ben shuddered, a clear indication he'd much prefer to deal with a compound leg fracture than swatches and paint chips. "She asks my opinion, which is always the same."

"And that is?"

"If you like it, sweetheart, so do I. Or some variation of that."

"Smart man."

"So smart, in fact, I recognized that you deliberately changed the subject."

Alex thought his segue had been seamless and unnoticeable. Obviously he'd been wrong. "I have no idea what you're talking about."

"Ellie," Ben reminded him cheerfully.

He was enjoying this way too much. Or it could be retribution for the way Alex had mercilessly ribbed him during a rough patch in his relationship with Cam.

Or there could be another reason.

"What about Ellie?"

"How's she doing?"

"You saw her on the way over here," Alex reminded him. "What's your professional opinion of how she is?"

"Looks like she's getting along fine, but I don't live with her."

It didn't come as a surprise that Ben knew of the arrangement. No way Sydney would keep the information to herself. This was as good a time as any to ask the question. "Did Syd put you up to this spontaneous visit?"

"What?" Ben was trying too hard to look innocent and he wasn't a very good actor.

"You know what. Getting juicy tidbits about Ellie and me."

"Are there any juicy tidbits to be had?"

Alex wanted to kick himself for walking right into that one. The fact that he and Ellie were having sex was a pretty significant tidbit and not one he planned to share. It was now his turn to pretend innocence. He would stick to the truth and avoid intimate details.

"Ellie is good company. Tidy."

"And not hard on the eyes," Ben added.

"Very true." Alex wished, not for the first time, that pretty was her only plus. But she was so much more than that. "And Martha says she doesn't put on airs. She's very down to earth."

Ben looked impressed. "That's an endorsement. Martha Spooner isn't easy to please."

"No kidding."

It was on the tip of his tongue but Alex stopped short of adding that the completion deadline for Mercy Medical Clinic had potentially been in jeopardy, except Ellie had pushed herself so that wouldn't happen. She had personal reasons, too, but hard work and resolve seemed part of her personality. It was hard to fake that. There was no quit in her.

"So there's nothing else you want to say?" Ben prodded.

He sure didn't want to mention those thoughts about Ellie to his brother. The word would spread and there'd be hell to pay, for sure. "Tell Sydney you did your best but couldn't wear me down."

"Do not tell her you figured it out," his brother demanded.

"Never. We have to stick together. Our sister is an annoying but well-intentioned meddler."

"She's protective."

"It runs in the family, or she couldn't have convinced you to do her dirty work." He had another thought. "Do you know why she's taking a break from dating?"

Ben shook his head. "She must have her reasons."

Join the club, Alex thought. "We need to set a good example and not try to get it out of her."

"In a perfect world that would work, but there are different rules for women."

"I know what you mean. As much as we'd like to ignore it, our sister is not a little girl anymore."

"Yeah," Ben said ruefully. "I think she knows we're there for her if she wants to talk."

"McKnights aren't notorious for sharing their feelings."

"I agree." He looked at his watch. "I also have to get back. Got patients waiting."

Alex nodded. "Thanks for stopping by."

At least for a little while he'd been distracted from wondering why he was more tense since having sex with Ellie. Now they had an agreement for nothing more than a fling. It would end when she left Blackwater Lake, and he planned to hold her to the pact.

But now he was thinking about something else. There was no quit in her, but did that extend to interpersonal relationships? Would she put all that grit and gumption into a commitment and stick with it no matter what?

Again he wanted to put his fist through a wall, because this was a pointless mental exercise. He would never again risk putting his heart on the line after trusting a woman who'd made a fool out of him.

That was a mistake he wouldn't repeat.

If you let a woman in, she could get to the place in a man's soul where his feelings were stored. Once she planted roots, she'd own him. Alex wasn't going to be owned by anyone. Not ever again.

Chapter Nine

After work, as soon as they'd arrived back at the house, Alex disappeared into his home office "to make phone calls." Personally, Ellie got the feeling he was simply avoiding her. He'd been acting weird all afternoon, ever since that visit from his brother. She could hang out in the family room or guest room, but as lovely as both rooms were, neither held any appeal.

She dropped her purse on the table by the front door then "crutched" herself to the kitchen. Martha's car was out front, so she knew the housekeeper was still around. And so far there were no negative vibes from her about having an extra person in the house.

She thumped to a stop by the island where the woman was preparing food. "Hi."

Martha never looked up. "Word of advice, Ellie. Don't quit your day job and be a cat burglar."

"You heard me coming?"

"A mile away." The older woman glanced up, her blue eyes twinkling. "But there are some, shall we say, athletic pursuits that don't require stealth and silence."

She was talking about sex and even if that wasn't what she meant, it was where Ellie's mind went. Plus, the woman worked here. There were things a person would have to be clueless not to notice, things that pointed to the fact she'd spent the past few nights in Alex's bed. This went under the heading of "Not Thinking It Through," and her face burned with embarrassment.

"Martha, it's not what you think—"

"So you and Alex aren't sleeping together?" She glanced up from slicing celery. A stainless-steel, copper-bottomed pot full of boiled potatoes and other vegetables waited close by.

"Okay, then it is what you think. But we have an agreement. It's not serious. After all, I'm leaving when Mercy Medical Clinic is finished."

"I only have four things to say about that." She glanced up for a moment. "One—when sex is involved, agreements don't usually work out. Two—Alex is always serious, ever since his mom died. Three—there are reasons why he doesn't 'go out' with women from Blackwater Lake. And four—you don't strike me as the sort of person who goes to bed with a man just for fun, and by that I mean without any feelings for him."

"Hmm." She really hoped Martha was wrong about that. In any event, there was nothing to be done about it now. "Can we talk about something else?"

"Anything you want."

"If I had to guess, I'd say you're making potato salad."

"Aren't you the rocket scientist," Martha teased. "Alex requested this to go with the steaks he's going to throw on the grill for dinner." She looked up quickly. "Please tell

me you're not one of those vegans who doesn't eat anything with eyes except potatoes."

"Are you kidding? I'm from Texas."

"Okay, then."

"Is there anything I can do to help you?"

"Sure. You can peel these suckers." She pointed to
where the potatoes waited. "I always make too many. But
there's a condition."

"What?" Stop sleeping with Alex?

"Sit down on that stool before you hurt yourself."

Ellie did as ordered, and Martha brought over a paring
knife, old newspaper for the peels and the full pot of spuds.

"How long have you been with Alex?" she asked.

"Since he moved back from California with that pregnant woman."

Not wife, Ellie thought. She looked up and there was a
sour, disapproving twist to Martha's mouth. "You didn't
like his wife?"

"No."

"Before or after she left Alex to go back with her child's
father?"

"He told you." It wasn't a question. She took a dill
pickle from the jar and tapped excess juice on the inside.
"Before. After she left, I wanted to cut her heart out with
an ice cream scoop."

That visual could turn a person against any frozen,
scoopable treat. "Wow, that would hurt a lot."

"That's the point."

"Should I be worried?" Ellie teased.

"Only if you're planning to break his heart."

"I'd never do that. Any more than he's planning to break
mine. I like and respect him too much to do that."

Martha met her gaze, took her measure then nodded.
"I believe you."

"Good." Ellie set a peeled potato in the provided bowl. "How long have you lived in Blackwater Lake?"

"Born and raised here. You'll never get me to say how many years ago that was."

"I'd guess thirty-nine."

"You would if you're as smart as I think you are." The housekeeper flashed a grin.

"So you knew Alex when he was a boy?"

"Yup. His mom was good people. I knew her pretty well. Sure hit that family hard when she died. Tom Mc-Knight could barely cope with his business. Alex took over raising his brother, and Sydney was just an infant. Folks in town took care of her while their dad was at work. Myself included."

"That was nice of you."

"Not just me and not particularly nice. It's what people do here. And I never married or had children, so I really enjoyed that baby girl." There was a soft expression in her pale blue eyes, as if she remembered it all. "When his sister got big enough, Alex raised her, too."

Ellie figured that's what she'd meant about him always being serious. Serious could be good because he was very serious in bed. The things he did to her body, how easily he made her want, should be illegal from coast to coast.

It was way past time for her to change the subject and put this conversation on neutral territory. "What do you think about the bazillionaire who wants to build a summer and winter resort here in Blackwater Lake? I hear he's a playboy.""

"That's the rumor," Ellie said.

"I guess I think there are pros and cons," Martha answered cryptically.

"Such as?"

"On the upside, that will bring a lot of money and people here. They need housing, goods and services. That kind of cash could do a lot of good in this community."

"But?"

"It will bring a lot of people in and life will change unless the powers that be don't have one eye on the bottom line and the other on keeping in balance what makes this place special."

Ellie nodded. "I know what you mean."

"And then there's my kitchen."

"Because you feel the need to feed all the newcomers?" It beat the heck out of her what that remark meant. "I'm sorry, but what does your kitchen have to do with a new resort?"

"Everything, if Adam gets the contracting job for it. They'll bring in their own contractor but will need to coordinate with an expert in this area."

"So he's being considered for the job. But I still don't get how that impacts you."

"He's been promising to remodel my kitchen ever since he came back to town. If he goes to work for the bazillionaire, he won't have time. Again."

"I see your point." Ellie peeled the last potato, then wiped her hands on the dishrag beside her. "What's wrong with your kitchen?"

"Too small." Martha wrinkled her nose with distaste. "It's narrow, like an apartment, and completely cut off from the great room, so the cook can't socialize."

Ellie guessed this woman would count it a real hardship to not be able to talk. "What else?"

"There's not enough storage, and the pantry's about as big as a postage stamp."

There was a pencil and pad of paper on the island with the beginning of a grocery list on it. Ellie tore off the top sheet, then made some bold lines, drawing what she imagined Martha's kitchen to be as the other woman chattered on. She sketched the wall above the sink knocked out so that when Martha was preparing food, she wasn't cut off socially. Obviously, without measurements or a visual this was all off the top of her head and not to scale, but she found room for a walk-in pantry and plenty of cupboards.

"What's that?" Martha's tone was equal parts curiosity and skepticism.

"Just something that popped into my head while you were talking. Do you want to see?"

"Sure."

Ellie turned the pad toward her and explained what she'd drawn. "Since I've never been inside your house, this isn't your kitchen, but—"

"Sure looks like it." The housekeeper inspected the drawing more closely. "That's three times as many cupboards as I've got now."

Her assumption was that Martha's house was older and from the description she'd guessed about the style. "This is all coming from my imagination. It's really rough—"

"Can you find room in there for a double oven and a bigger refrigerator?"

"Measurements would need to be taken, and you're working with a finite amount of space. It could be that you'd have to sacrifice some of the cupboards to do that. Compromise is a must, and only the client can decide what's most important to them."

The other woman looked impressed. "Do you do that drawing stuff for a whole house, too?"

"Yes, ma'am. I can do it for pretty much any building. When you're starting from scratch it's a longer process. There are a lot of meetings to figure out what the customer wants, and at that stage nothing is carved in stone.

It's exciting when you can capture exactly what a person has been trying to put into words."

"Well, honey, you sure got mine right. You must have a gift for it."

"Listening is important. But now computers are an indispensable tool in the process. I can create a three-dimensional image to really see what the finished product is going to look like."

"Make sure your customer can picture the real thing when living there," the housekeeper mused.

"Exactly."

Not unlike her current situation with Alex, she thought. The two of them were sleeping together, to be totally honest. More than roommates, but not a couple. They occupied space under the same roof, and by any interpretation that was called living together. But she was definitely getting a picture of what the real thing could be.

So far it had been great. In bed, Alex made her heart pound and her skin tingle. At work during the day she could hardly wait for quitting time when they went to his house together. He was funny and generous, and he'd taken care of her when she'd needed him. But only because he needed her, too. By mutual consent, when they didn't need each other any longer, this living-together thing would be over.

Part of her didn't want it to end, but the practical part knew that was inevitable. Having the rules spelled out ahead of time should have brought peace of mind, but that wasn't how she felt. Every day that went by made her less sure about being able to walk away with her heart unscathed.

Whatever was going on between her and Alex went against everything she'd learned and all the training she'd had becoming an architect. Unlike the structures she designed, this relationship wasn't built to last.

"Alex?"

At the sound of Ellie's soft voice, he looked up from the building supply list he'd been studying. She was standing in the doorway of his office balancing on the crutches.

The most absurd thought crossed his mind. There were rubber pads on the curved part, but when you used it to take body weight, there had to be discomfort. "Do those things hurt your arms?"

She glanced down to where her hands curved on the horizontal hold. "Not much anymore."

That meant it did at first and she'd never once complained. Just one more thing to respect. To like.

She was wearing denim shorts and a T-shirt that said Blackwater Lake, Montana, on the front. It matched the hot-pink cast on her leg. All of a sudden he wanted her, and the feeling was so big, so deep, so consuming there wasn't room for anything else.

"Are you still working?" she asked.

"Not really."

"Getting hungry?"

She didn't mean it as a loaded question, but he took it that way because of where his mind was. He was hungry for her, and he hadn't been working even before she came in because he couldn't stop thinking about her.

"I could eat," he finally said.

"Martha made potato salad. I helped," she added. "But don't worry, it was grunt work. She said you were going to barbecue steaks."

"Yeah." Then a thought struck him. "You're not a vegetarian, are you?"

"Why do y'all keep asking me that? I'm from Texas."

"Good."

"You've seen me eat meat."

He grinned. A woman after his own heart. Well, not after it, because he'd made clear that it wasn't part of their agreement. This was about having fun, and that's what he was going to do.

He stood. "Let's get dinner going."

"About dang time." She quickly backed up and maneuvered toward the kitchen.

"You're getting pretty good on those things."

"I know. Wanna race?" She glanced over her shoulder and grinned.

"I'm afraid you'd win."

"Like everything else, practice makes perfect." She stopped and looked at him. "But when I get this pink plastic piece of torture off, I hope I never have to use this skill again."

"Is the cast hurting?"

"No. My leg itches. Ben warned me not to try and slide anything down there to scratch it, because that usually doesn't end well."

"My brother, the orthopedist, should know."

Alex sort of missed carrying her around. At first it had been a chance to hold her, but now with their current arrangement he held her every night. Still, he liked picking her up; she was small and delicate and... He couldn't explain the feeling because it would make him sound like a caveman. Just thinking this made him feel stupid.

In the kitchen doorway Ellie stopped. "Do you want me to set the table?"

"Why don't we eat outside?" The idea was spontaneous, and he wasn't sure where it came from.

"That sounds wonderful." Her delighted smile made him feel as if he'd just handed her the moon.

"I'll carry everything to the patio and you can arrange it on the table." She nodded and he added, "What else did Martha fix?"

"Green salad, corn on the cob in foil and berries with cream for dessert."

"Let's get this show on the road. I'm starving." He hoped she didn't notice him staring at her mouth when he said that.

It took a few trips in and out to get everything, and Ellie kept apologizing for not being able to help more. He didn't mind. The company was a rare treat, and he'd enjoy it for the time being.

While he grilled the filets and corn, she arranged place mats and plates on the round redwood table for four situated on the covered patio. Up against the house there was a matching wooden love seat and chairs with padded seats that formed a conversation area.

The back grass stretched out for an acre to the forest of fir trees that was a natural property line. Bushes and flowers ringed the perimeter of the yard and looked just about perfect, which wasn't bragging, in his humble opinion.

When the food was cooked, he put it on the platter and turned off the propane barbecue, then brought everything to the table where Ellie was already sitting.

"Yum, that smells good. I tossed the salad. Hope y'all like ranch dressing."

"Works for me."

The sun was just descending in the sky and would drop behind the mountains soon, but for now there was enough light. They ate in silence for a while, which was a good thing because every time he looked at her mouth, slick from eating buttered corn, he felt as if he'd swallowed his tongue. Worse, he wanted to kiss the slickness from her lips.

It was a relief when Ellie took a bite of potato salad. "Mmm. I can't believe how good this is."

"One of my housekeeper's specialties."

"You got lucky when she came to work for you."

"The McKnight family got lucky with neighbors way before that."

"Yeah." She met his gaze. "She told me about taking care of your baby sister while your dad worked."

"Everyone pitched in to help. That's just the way Blackwater Lake people roll."

Ellie cleared her throat and looked down. "Martha knows we're sharing a bed...room," she added.

"That doesn't surprise me."

The woman noticed everything. While he hadn't taken that into consideration when he'd proposed their fling, it wouldn't have changed his mind. As much as he teased her about gossiping, he'd known Martha could be discreet when Ellie became more than a guest.

"And she knows about our 'athletic pursuits.'" If there was more light, the pink in her cheeks would be visible. There was no doubt it was there. "But I got her drift."

"Did she say anything else?"

"As I recall, she had about four points, none of which apply to us or our particular situation."

He heard something in her voice that told him she wasn't telling the whole truth. But he had a pretty good idea what his housekeeper had said. "Martha is outspoken."

"Yeah, I noticed."

"Did she upset you?" Alex couldn't imagine the woman being in any way mean, but firmness was another matter.

"No. She said, and let me paraphrase, if things don't go as planned, she'll cut my heart out with an ice cream scoop."

He figured her point had something to do with not hurting him, because he'd heard that threat in relation to his ex-wife. Still… "Ouch."

"No kidding." She laughed. "I appreciate where she's coming from. She embraced you and your siblings because she never had kids of her own. The three of you are like her children, and that explains her finely developed protective streak."

"It goes both ways."

"And that's the thing. I've noticed that people like Martha are the backbone of Blackwater Lake. It's a highlight of all that's so wonderful here."

"I couldn't agree more."

"Then I have to ask—how do you feel about the resort development? Other than having the work." She took a bite of steak and chewed.

"Good question." Alex thought for a moment. "I've got mixed emotions. On the one hand, I'd like to maintain the serene sort of isolated feel of the place where I grew up."

The place where he'd planned to raise his family.

"On the other hand," she said, "a resort as big as the one that's being proposed will all but assure Blackwater Lake is going to grow."

"Yeah. I've talked with the representatives for the developer who's spearheading the deal, and we're looking at a small airport in addition to hotels, restaurants and stores."

Ellie's look was wry. "I'm in favor of an airport, although no one asked for my opinion."

"I figured." He grinned, remembering her first day on the job when she was late after driving nearly a hundred miles from "that cute little airport." "Financial success relies on tourists, and they need to be able to get here without too much trouble."

"Common sense," she agreed.

"If the city council approves the plan and permits are pulled, there's no way things around here won't change."

"Not all of them will be bad," she pointed out. "The clinic is already expanding. Probably that kind of growth will require a hospital be built. And for you personally, if you're the chosen contractor, that would be an incredible triumph for McKnight Construction."

"Yeah." He'd thought about all of that. "And money buys road improvements, infrastructure enhancement. All changes for the better. Including creating a lot of jobs."

"Compromise can mean the best of all possible worlds here."

"True," he agreed. "From your mouth to God's ear, because I think it's going to happen."

"I'm full." Ellie put down her fork and leaned back in the chair, indicating this was about eating and not the conversation. She sighed as a light breeze stirred the hair around her face. "The thing is, I'm sure there's a way to incorporate change and still maintain the qualities that make this area so amazing and incredibly special."

He hadn't been aware that she noticed or felt so strongly. "Like what?"

"The trees. I can smell the pine and it's wonderful." She breathed it in. "I've never seen more magnificent mountains. Although, keeping it real, Texas is pretty flat."

"I've heard that."

"I thought the sky at home was pretty, but here…" She shook her head, as if she were at a loss for words.

"What?"

"It's clear to me why this is called Big Sky country. During the day, the vivid blue takes your breath away. But only until twilight. Like now." Wonder transformed her face. It was an expression that couldn't be faked. "This gets into your soul and doesn't want to leave. Then at night the stars are like glitter on velvet."

The sentiment made him proud about his hometown and pleased that she got it. His ex had done nothing but complain about being stuck out in the middle of nowhere. "That's poetic."

"It's the God's-honest truth. The sky, the trees, the grass, the flowers." She looked completely relaxed when she waved a hand to indicate his house, yard and the jagged, towering mountains beyond. "I could get used to this."

It was silent for a moment, then she tensed, as if what she'd said sank in. "I didn't mean *here* here. Just Montana in general."

"I knew that."

"Good. Because—"

"It's okay, Ellie."

But it wasn't. Not completely. The idea of it made him uneasy. The pleasure of her enjoyment and approval trickled through him in a way that meant it mattered a lot to him that she liked Blackwater Lake, the area and his place. Her opinion, good or bad, shouldn't mean anything to him. She was leaving and he had no intention of stopping her, but...

There was always a *but,* and he had a bad feeling this one meant her not being here would make him awful damn lonely.

Chapter Ten

Ellie left the Mercy Medical Clinic site and walked back to the construction trailer. The crutches barely slowed her down now, but hopping upstairs to an apartment would still be a challenge. It wasn't clear how much of that rationalization was based on the fact that she liked living with Alex and she refused to analyze the situation too closely. Things were good, professionally and personally, and she wanted to keep it that way.

She'd been in town almost six weeks already and had been at his place for nearly four. A few more and her work here would be done, then she'd go back to Texas. The thought made her sad and wistful, but determined to enjoy the time she had left. She had no excuse to stay longer.

Unless he asked her to stay. The idea had more appeal than she would have liked and about as much chance of happening as pigs flying.

She pushed the trailer door inward and held it with her shoulder while maneuvering herself inside. "Hi."

Alex looked up from the work on his desk. "Hey. What's going on?"

"The smoke detectors and fire alarms installation is on schedule and testing is projected for a couple days from now. If all goes well it should be ready for inspection. And the crew is going home for the day."

"Good."

She looked more closely and noticed that his desk was overflowing with files and paper that looked out of proportion to the current job, especially since it was winding down.

"What are you working on?"

"Juggling," he said ruefully.

She moved in front of him and leaned on the crutches to keep her weight off the healing leg. "You must be really good, because keeping three pieces of paper in the air is like trying to catch the wind."

"Not literally." He leaned back in his chair, but the tension was still plain in the tightness of his shoulders. "I'm looking at scenarios if the resort project becomes a reality. If my bid to be the contractor is accepted, I need to make sure I can supply the crews necessary to meet those deadlines along with the obligations I already have."

"What else is going on?" She sat on a chair in front of his desk.

"I've got some land around the lake where I'm building custom homes. Just finished one for Ben." He grinned. "Fortunately his fiancée loves it, too."

"So this isn't a tract?"

He shook his head. "Custom. Potential clients can pick out a site and buy the land, then hire their own architect to draw up plans. Then we build."

"That sounds exciting."

"Yeah." His frown said something else altogether. "I have some of my own money invested, so there's a personal and financial stake in this for me. And people who want a home don't want to wait until a big undertaking like the resort is complete to get their house built."

"I see what you mean. Hence, the juggling."

He nodded. "I may have to recruit construction people from out of the area. Possibly from out of state, too. So I'm looking into how feasible it is."

"Y'all have a lot riding on this. But what an adventure. Watching the town where you grew up making progress like that. And being lucky enough to participate in it."

For the first time he smiled. "Yeah."

"It just hit me that other than the town, the only part of Blackwater Lake I've seen is what's around the marina."

A tour of that body of water had been the last thing on her mind while he was taking a tour of her body on his boat.

Alex looked thoughtful. "Are we finished for the day?"

"The crew has probably left. I don't have anything. Can't speak for you."

He reached into his top drawer and pulled out the truck keys. "Let's go see the lake and I'll give you the two-cent tour."

"I'd love it." And just the word *tour* made tingles dance down her spine.

Fifteen minutes later they were on the winding road circling the tree-covered mountain that overlooked Blackwater Lake. Alex pointed out where his property started and ended, an extraordinary parcel.

"The lots are already staked out and I've even sold a few. Some buyers are holding on to it as an investment, and others are looking for architects and anticipate starting construction after getting all their ducks in a row."

Watching ducks paddling around on the lake's surface, she smiled. "That's an appropriate expression, what with this fantastic view of those cute little fowl treading water."

"Are ducks fowl?" he asked.

"I'm sure they are, what with those feathers everywhere and various other functions they don't bother to control."

He rolled his eyes. "Very funny."

"I try." She looked at the water and sighed in wonder. "That is a breathtaking view."

She stared out at the blue ripples of the lake, knowing it was a reflection of the cloudless sky above. The angle of the sun's rays sparkled on the swells and turned them to diamonds. On the far side, towering, rugged mountains carved out a dark silhouette in the sky.

"Wow, simply amazing." She glanced at the scenery they were passing, where homes would sit. "The exterior design of a structure is always important, but more so here."

"Why?"

"First of all there has to be a lot of windows. Missing out on a view of the lake or mountains has got to be illegal in Montana." Thoughtfully she tapped her lip. "You'd want to preserve as many trees as possible and make sure that any left are far enough from the structure that limbs wouldn't damage it in a windstorm. Or snow."

"Because the branches get heavy and could break." He sounded a little surprised she would know that.

"Right," she said, her mind still going a mile a minute. She pointed to the lot they were driving by. "I could see a mountain-lodge-type place there. Maybe with dormers. Depending on what view appeals to the client, the master bedroom could be in the front, on the lake. Or on the back, looking at the mountains. Decks on both sides, depending on which view they're in the mood for."

"That's a good point."

"And there." She pointed at the next lot. "A stone front with wooden pillars. Imposing in a woodsy way. A sentinel where the lake narrows just there. Where you'd make a stand if defense was a priority."

"I see what you mean."

"Nothing too modern here," she mused. "It would stand out like a bump on a pickle, and that shouldn't be. Any building should blend, enhance, and this forest and lake have been here for hundreds, maybe thousands of years. It isn't modern architecture friendly."

"Wow."

She glanced over, wondering if she should be embarrassed. "I'm sorry. Didn't mean to blather on."

"On the contrary. Blather away. I'm very impressed."

She didn't want to glow at his words, but just couldn't help herself. "I'll be sure to add blathering to the work history and skill set on my résumé."

"That wasn't a joke, Ellie. You have a flair for orientation and a good artistic eye that complements your innate common sense. I can visualize what you just said, and it's exactly what I had in mind when I bought the land."

His approval was balm to her battered and bruised confidence. How fun how would it be to work with one of Alex's buyers on a house design. Taking the thought a step further: how much fun it would be to work with *him*. The words were on the tip of her tongue but she held back.

She loved architecture, drawing up plans and watching a structure take shape from her ideas and vision. Her talent, or lack of it, wasn't what had derailed her career. A bad personal choice was responsible for that. Personal decisions had no place in the business world, and she'd paid a high price for that lesson.

As long as she was sharing Alex's bed, work decisions fell in the personal column, and she needed to remember that. Suddenly she felt a little nauseated. Probably from this winding road. Or the surge of creative ideas threatening to make her head implode. Either way her stomach wasn't happy.

Her cell phone rang and she pulled it from her purse. Caller ID said Lincoln Hart. She looked over at Alex. "Sorry, I have to take this."

She wasn't sorry, and she didn't really have to take it. She was relieved at the interruption. "Hi, Linc."

"Hey, baby sister. How y'all doin'?"

"Good. You?"

"Calling for my daily update. So let the update commence."

"I get this cast off in a couple of days."

She felt more than saw Alex glance at her and wondered if that was a happy reminder for him. Would he be glad to get rid of her? Was he doing the internal dance of joy because she would be out of his hair soon? There was another weird feeling in her stomach that wasn't nausea, but the pathetic hope that he wouldn't be glad, that he would miss her. Because she knew she was going to miss him.

"Wish I could see you in a cast. Is it pink?"

"My favorite color. I could text you a picture, but there's no way. Y'all would find a way to make me regret it."

"It's too easy, sis. You're just very fertile ground for teasing."

"Believe me, I'm trying to change that."

Alex cleared his throat. "Do you need to stop anywhere before we head home?"

If there was a God in heaven, her brother had not just heard that. "So, what's up there?"

"Nice try. Suellen Hart, is there a man with you?"

"Yes." This didn't have to be bad.

"Do you want to tell me about him?"

"Not really."

"Please say this isn't someone you work with," her brother said.

"If only."

"Ellie, is this the coworker who drove you to the hospital? The one you led me to believe was a she?"

"You've got that right." She smiled brightly at Alex.

"I smell trouble. Do I need to come down there?"

"Of course not." And that's all she was going to say. "Gotta run, Linc. Love you." She clicked off before he could say more, get her to say more and figure out Alex hadn't just taken care of her, but she'd been living with him.

Getting back to her own place couldn't happen soon enough to suit her. The longer she spent under Alex's roof, the worse it would be when she left. Just minutes ago she'd come close to wishing for more even though she knew it was a pipe dream. How could she forget he'd spelled out the rules in advance. His boat was named *Independence,* for goodness' sake.

If she got hurt, there'd be no putting it on him. It wasn't as if he'd lied, or promised or hadn't warned her. No, this time she would have no one to blame but herself.

Alex was off somewhere checking on one of his crews while Ellie held down the fort. At the Mercy Medical Clinic project, the plumbing, electrical and specialty preparation for medical equipment was completed and inspected, and the rest of the work would go pretty fast.

Being in the construction trailer by herself was both good and bad. She liked having Alex in the same room when they worked or talked, laughed and teased. But he'd looked weird when she'd said how easy it would be to get used to the beauty and serenity of Montana. The weirdness had continued today. He'd been standoffish and kept his distance since the night of the lovely dinner outside and even more so after showing her his property around the lake.

If a rewind-and-delete were possible, she would take back the words that were making him jumpy. Now he was acting as if she'd proposed they live together permanently. Or declared her love. She knew better than that. She'd helped write the rules of the fling.

The trailer door opened and kept her from working herself into a snit. Another good thing—the door opener wasn't Alex. Jill Beck and Adam Stone walked in. Technically they were now Dr. and Mrs. Stone, the handsome dark-haired doctor and his perky, redheaded wife.

"Hey, it's the newlyweds." She started to grab her crutches to stand.

"Don't get up." Adam held out his hand to stop her as the couple moved closer to her desk.

"Okay." She relaxed into the chair. "I haven't seen you two since the wedding. How was the Tahiti trip?"

Jill's eyes sparkled. "Fabulous. I can't think of any words to describe it adequately."

"I can." Adam slid his arm around her waist and drew his wife closer against his side. "Sun, sand, clear blue ocean and Jill in a bikini. Life just does not get any better. Unless you want to hear about how awesome married life is now that we're home."

"That is actually a pretty good description," Ellie admitted.

"So when are you coming back to the apartment?" Jill asked. "I feel awful that we weren't here for you, and now you're paying rent on a place you can't even use."

"The cast is coming off in a few days, Ben says. I'll move back then."

"How is it staying with Alex?" Jill was trying very hard to put idle interest into her tone, but there was an undercurrent of feminine curiosity that every woman understood.

"I don't know what I'd have done without him. He's been a really good friend."

And so much more.

"How good is good?" Jill put her hand over her mouth and glanced up at her husband. "Sorry. I'm being nosy. I so didn't mean to actually say that out loud."

"Yes, she did." The doctor grinned. "It's not like the whole town of Blackwater Lake put her up to being the one to find out the truth. But in the interest of full disclosure, you should know that inquiring minds are trying to figure out whether or not Alex has a girlfriend."

"Because no one can remember him dating a local girl," Jill added. "There's a rumor but no proof that he goes out of town for his—needs."

The town assumed right, Ellie thought, but it wasn't her job to confirm or deny. This was just the sort of thing he wanted to avoid. If no one knew about his personal life, feelings couldn't be hurt. Business wouldn't suffer.

Ellie looked up at Dr. and Mrs. Stone and put the blankest, most innocent possible expression on her face. "I have a hunch the two of you have another reason for stopping by today."

"Okay. I'll take that as a very diplomatic way of saying mind your own business," Jill said. "And I apologize in advance for whoever asks you the questions next time. And there will be a next time."

"We actually do have a reason for stopping by," Adam said. "Jill came to the clinic to have lunch with me today—"

"It doesn't happen often," his wife said. "But I ran into Martha Spooner at the market and she told me about the wonderful ideas you had for her kitchen remodel and how you just drew it up on a napkin."

"It was actual paper." Ellie was pleased at the compliment.

"Adam and I are talking about building a house."

"Really?" Ellie was surprised, since their place on the marina at Blackwater Lake seemed like it suited them. "What about the property where you are now? Will you rent out upstairs and down?"

"Actually, I'm going to sell it. I had a really good offer on it."

"And the apartment?"

"The buyer is a novelist. Pretty famous. He wanted a quiet place by the water. Said something about a second home, but I got the impression it was for solitude when he's working. He said something about making the upstairs an office, but he definitely won't rent it out. Said he doesn't need the income or aggravation."

"So, I'm being evicted?" Ellie teased.

"At the rate the clinic expansion is moving along, you'll be gone long before the sale goes through."

"So you accepted the offer?"

Jill nodded. "He's paying cash. There's a signed contract and open escrow. A lawyer is handling the details and said it doesn't look like there will be a problem."

Ellie looked at each of them in turn. "So you need a house."

"Yeah. Although it's a scary proposition." Jill slid her

hands into the pockets of her jeans. "What if it's all finished and we hate it?"

Ellie thought it was an exciting plan. A new home to start off their brand-new life together.

"We've looked at property in Alex's custom home development overlooking the lake and mountains."

"I've been through there. It's breathtaking." She envied this couple, so much in love. You could almost see an aura around them.

"We thought so." Jill was practically quivering with excitement. "Then I saw Martha, and since Adam and I were both here together, we thought we could talk to you about ideas for a house."

"I'm happy to do that. But y'all know I'll be leaving and it will be necessary to find an architect to do the job."

"We're aware," the other woman said. "But at least we'll have some ideas at that point. We know you."

"We like you," Adam chimed in.

"So it's not intimidating to talk about this," Jill added.

"The experience should never be like that," Ellie explained. "If someone wants something hideous, it's my job to point it out and why. In the nicest, most diplomatic way possible. If the client chooses to ignore the warning, there's not much to do except build what they want."

"That's why we thought it would be good to start the planning process with someone we trust."

Jill's hopeful expression reminded Ellie of her seven-year-old son, C.J. It would be really hard to say no to that face. Fortunately, she very much wanted to help them out.

"Okay. Have a seat." She hadn't offered before, figuring they'd only be there a short time. After pulling out a sketch pad she used for rough drawings, she asked, "Any idea how big a house you want?"

"In that development, I think there's a minimum square-footage requirement." Adam leaned an elbow on the desk. "Ben McKnight's house is about thirty-five hundred, give or take. We were thinking of that as a starting point."

Ellie nodded. "You can always make the footprint bigger depending on the number of rooms and the size of them. And until you decide on a lot, you really can't make firm decisions on the final size."

"We want a big yard for C.J.," Adam said.

"So you're probably going to want a two-story. The smaller foundation will leave more land." She looked at them. "Family size should be taken into consideration."

"We want three more kids." Jill smiled. "C.J. needs three siblings, to make an even number of children."

"Okay. Five bedrooms. I'm thinking the master should have room for a nursery that eventually can be turned into a parents' retreat."

"That sounds wonderful."

"A home office for you, Doctor?"

He looked at his wife, then nodded. "As much as I'd like to leave my work at work, practicing medicine isn't like any other profession. Patients call. There's paperwork. And at least I could do it under the same roof as my family. So, yes to the office."

"Okay." Ellie nodded thoughtfully as ideas for the house came to her. "I'm thinking downstairs study close to the family room that should have a flat-screen TV and fireplace."

"Sounds wonderful." Jill tapped her lip as she looked at her husband. "How do you feel about formal living and dining rooms?"

"That's up to you."

Good answer, Ellie thought.

"Then I say yes," his wife answered.

"I saw your family at the wedding, Adam. They all live out of town."

He nodded. "My brother is in Las Vegas, my parents live in Dallas, your neck of the woods. My sister's family is in Houston."

"So you'll probably have visitors and will be needing guest rooms. A big laundry room with a sink and hanging space for clothes."

"It's sounding really big." Jill looked worried.

"We don't want to go too small then have to move." Adam's look was tender. "And you're concerned about cost. I know that look, honey. But we can afford whatever will make you happy."

Ellie wanted to sigh. What a great guy. Alex would be, too, if he'd ever loosen up and take a chance. She ignored that feeling as best as she could while concentrating on sketching. The young couple on the other side of her desk talked quietly about Jill's inclination to lean on the conservative side and Adam's to make her happy.

She took a ruler from the drawer beside her and drew bold lines for the first and second floors, then blocked off the rooms. Picturing a spacious entry, she put twin curving staircases in it with formal living on the left and a dining room to the right. Behind it was a kitchen large enough for lots of kids, pantry with enough space to keep provisions for a family of ten, just in case. Two guest rooms with separate bathrooms.

Upstairs was for the family and an open room over the garage where kids could spread out to study and play when they could be more independent.

"Here's a rough drawing." She turned the pad for them to see and explained the layout, where she pictured fireplaces, a kitchen island, nook for the table and windows across the back for a view.

"Oh, Ellie—" Jill was speechless with excitement.

"Remember, nothing is carved in stone. No pun intended," she said to Adam.

"I've never heard that one before."

"Oh, sweetie, can't you just see this in your head? It's everything I want," his wife said.

"The architect you work with will probably have more ideas."

Ellie knew she would if she was the one doing the job from conception to completion. She liked Jill and Adam Stone and would have loved to design their new home, see the project through. But she wouldn't be there, and the thought made her sad. Later she would think about the fact that the feeling wasn't only about not designing this house.

Just then the door opened and Alex walked in. He took off the hard hat and ran his fingers through his hair. Worn denim hugged his hips and thighs and the black T-shirt tucked into the jeans highlighted his lean masculine strength. Her heart did that little skip thing that made her pulse pound, and if Jill and Adam hadn't been looking at him, they would have the answer to the question that the whole town wanted to know: Ellie and Alex were more than friends, and a lot had been going on since she'd moved into his house.

The two men shook hands and Alex said hello to Jill. "It's nice to see you. How was Tahiti?"

"Awesome," the two said together.

He saw the sketch on her desk. At the top she'd written their name and would start a file for them to take to whoever actually would draw up the plans.

"What's up?" he asked.

"We're buying a lot in your custom home development," Adam explained.

Alex glanced at her and his expression was impossible to read. "Ellie had a bunch of ideas for building there when I took her through. Where to pour foundations to preserve as many trees as possible. An orientation to get sun during the day."

"And she did a terrific sketch from the ideas we talked about just now. It took her about five minutes." Adam looked at her with sincere regret. "It's a darn shame you're not staying here in Blackwater Lake. The two of you would make a great team. She could design the houses for you to build."

This time Ellie understood the look on Alex's face and knew he didn't want to be on her team—or any other woman's, for that matter. Maybe it had something to do with this young couple and the happiness that radiated from them as they planned a future with a family, but the idea tugged at her heart in a way she'd never felt before.

That was bad with a capital *B*.

For the first time she was glad to be moving back to her apartment soon and grateful that the clinic addition was nearing completion. She really needed to go home before leaving Blackwater Lake could break her heart.

Chapter Eleven

"I knew the cast was coming off today after work. How could I forget my shoe?" Probably because she was usually waiting for the other shoe to fall and didn't want to give the universe more ammunition than it already had.

"If I were you, I'd think about waiting awhile to wear those four-inch heels again. Just saying…." Alex glanced over, then returned his gaze to the road that would take them out of town and back to his place. "How does the ankle feel?"

"Heavenly." She rotated her foot, trying to ignore the emaciated, anemic-looking liberated limb. The doctor had said she would lose muscle mass and it would take a while to come back, but she'd be good as new soon. "I don't miss the crutches. It still itches, but there are options without the cast—lotion and actual scratching."

"And I guess being able to put weight on it is a plus."

"It's funny how weird walking normally feels. I've been

doing it for a long time. Then a few weeks out of commission and bam—like a toddler again. On the positive side, climbing stairs will help build up my leg."

He glanced at her and the look was deliberately casual with overtones of intensity. "Since you're already settled in at my place, what do you think about staying on until the job is finished?"

The words were spoken so nonchalantly, it took several beats for the message to sink in. When it did, there was pounding in her head and ringing in her ears. He was asking her to stay with him, and joy bubbled up inside her. Then the finer point of it found the way to her heart.

Until the job is finished.

The subtext was that he wouldn't change his mind about this only being temporary. He might have relaxed his rule about sleeping with a woman in town, but his core belief hadn't altered. He wouldn't commit to a relationship.

She tried very hard not to be hurt. He'd never lied to her, not even once. But she liked him so much, and knowing he wouldn't let himself care brought the sting of tears to her eyes. Her emotions were just right there at the surface, and that wasn't like her at all. The challenge was not letting him see, because that would be so humiliating.

"Ellie?"

"Hmm?" She didn't trust her voice to be neutral, and that single sound was all she could manage.

"It makes sense for you to hang at my place."

"Why?"

It took him a moment to answer, and when he did, the tone was guarded. "Your things are already there."

"I can move them back." It wasn't all that much.

"Then there's the fact that we have fun."

"Are you trying to say you'll miss me?"

He glanced at her, then returned his gaze to the road. "I will. When you go back to Texas."

Since he always told the truth, that was something, at least, but she wanted more. More than he could give. The sooner she made the break, the sooner she could keep herself from barreling into whatever crash was heading her way if she didn't get off this particular path.

"That's very sweet of you, Alex. But it's time for me to get back to my place. I've inconvenienced you long enough."

The glance he gave her was ironic, but his mouth pulled tight before he spoke. "Yeah, you've been tough to take."

"Being difficult is a dirty job, but someone has to do it." She was trying to pull off breezy and clever instead of whiny and sad, which was how she really felt.

"I'll miss that sass when you go back to Texas."

Give me a reason to stay, she silently pleaded. She would miss more than sass. She'd miss falling asleep in his arms and waking up with him in the morning. She'd miss the sex, too, but the closeness was deep and satisfying and safe. It was easy and spontaneous and something she'd never experienced before. Since he didn't say more, she figured it was only that way for her. She was looking out the truck window when a single tear slid down her cheek and he gave no indication of noticing.

A half hour later Alex was barricaded in his home office and Ellie had her suitcase open in the master bedroom, on the tufted bench at the foot of the bed. She'd changed into jeans and sneakers. The left one felt strange, but that would get better. So would the pain inside that had nothing to do with breaking her ankle.

She'd taken her things out of the drawer in his dresser where he'd made room when they'd agreed on a fling. Her makeup and other toiletries were in the bathroom, and she was just walking out with them when Martha came into the room.

"Look at you," the housekeeper said. "Moving on two good legs."

Ellie set the things in the suitcase then watched the older woman put a pile of clothes on the bed. Obviously none of it was Alex's, and her efforts were appreciated.

"Are you proud of me?" Ellie asked.

"Maybe. Maybe not."

She noticed a chill in the voice and the way Martha's mouth looked all pinchy and tight. The older woman had been nothing but warm and friendly since that first moment they'd met in Alex's home office. When she had said to Martha "Please call me Ellie," it was as if she'd passed some sort of test, but now she was flunking and didn't understand why.

Ellie sat on the bed, her leg aching a little. "Have I done something wrong?"

"Not yet, as far as I can tell."

Yet? That meant there was potential.

"Y'all are looking at me as if I substituted olive oil for your favorite window cleaner. Something's going on, but I'm not sure what it is. Unless you tell me, I can't fix it."

And she very much wanted to do that at least.

"You and Alex seem pretty—close—in every way. If you know what I'm saying."

Ellie did know and she knew Martha knew. It would have been impossible not to notice; the woman wasn't an idiot. To her credit, the housekeeper hadn't breathed a word of the arrangement; otherwise, Jill and Adam wouldn't have been asking questions the day they'd dropped by the construction trailer.

Still, Ellie tried to choose her words carefully. "Alex has been a good friend to me when I very much needed one."

"So that's all? Just friends?" Eyes that missed nothing narrowed, as if that was the wrong answer.

"It's all he wants. But I have to admit that I'm going to miss him very much when I leave Blackwater Lake."

"Funny you should say that. In my humble opinion something else is missing." One eyebrow lifted questioningly.

Now Ellie was completely at a loss. "I'm not sure what you mean."

"Then I'll spell it out." The glitter in her eyes was just shy of a glare. "You've been living in this house a little over a month."

"Yes, I'm well aware of that. But—"

Martha held up a hand. "I'm not prying, but I do notice things. I cook and it seems to me that you're not eating very much. Do you feel all right?"

"Yes. Mostly. But sometimes the smell of food makes me feel sick and my appetite goes missing."

There was a knowing gleam in the older woman's eyes when she asked, "Are you missing anything else?"

"Mising anything?" Then the meaning sank in.

Missing, as in her period. Dear Lord, the woman was right. She hadn't had… "Oh my God—"

"I see the light's come on."

"A baby?"

"That's what *pregnant* means."

If she hadn't already been sitting, Ellie probably would have collapsed as the shock rushed in. She felt like the world's biggest moron. But there had been so much on her plate since that night on Alex's boat. He'd told her the condom broke, but seriously? It was only one time. What were the odds? Apparently a hundred percent.

Now it made sense. Her stomach was upset in the morning and she was unbelievably tired. Now that she thought about it, her breasts were sore. Seems as if she'd heard somewhere that was an indicator.

"I don't know what to say."

"So you had no idea?" There was skepticism in the housekeeper's voice.

"I know it's hard to believe. But, no. It didn't cross my mind this could happen. It always happens to someone else." She'd put it out of her mind because there was a job to be done. She broke her ankle. Then moved in with Alex. It was a lot to process. But she should have been more aware. "I'm an idiot."

"The thing is," Martha said, "it's no skin off my nose if you are or aren't. Pregnant, I mean, not an idiot. But his ex—Mrs. McKnight—lied to him. Letting him think he was the father to that baby of hers hurt him deep down where a man is most at risk. And he's never gotten over it. You need to find out if you're carrying his child and tell him. *Before* you leave town."

Ellie nodded. "I would never keep something like that from him. I care about Alex." Even if she didn't, the honorable thing would be to let him know if he was going to be a father.

"I didn't think you'd do any less. But I feel real protective of him and had to say something. I believe you know as well as I do that he's a good man. He'll figure it all out and do the right thing."

Ellie's stomach knotted when she realized this was the other shoe to fall. She needed to find out right away whether or not it was a ballet slipper or a combat boot that was going to smack her.

When Ellie had wished Alex would give her a reason to stay in Blackwater Lake, a baby was not what she'd had in mind. She looked at the drugstore bag on the pas-

senger seat beside her. Inside it was a pregnancy test kit.
Two actually—different brands, just to be thorough. She'd
picked them up after work, which had been more stress-
ful than usual, since she was trying to act as if her life
wasn't in crisis. Now she was on her way to her rented
apartment to find out if *crisis* was the right word to describe the state of her life.

On some level she'd realized her period was late, but
she'd figured that was a side effect of physical trauma and
the pressure of a new job. The stress and excitement of
living with Alex. As of yesterday she wasn't living with
him but somehow the stress was worse, and being pregnant wasn't what she'd call exciting.

She turned off the main road by the Quonset hut-shaped
mailboxes, then pulled into her parking space. Both Jill's
and Adam's cars were there, and she wasn't sure whether
or not that made what she had to do worse. After grab-
bing her bag off the seat, she headed toward the front of
the house. C.J. was in the front yard with a soccer ball.

"Hi, Ellie," he called out. "Watch me dribble."

"Okay." She knew enough about the sport to get that he
wasn't talking about drool. Moving closer, she saw him
carefully move the black-and-white ball with the side of
his foot. It wasn't pretty, but he was concentrating with
everything he had. "Good job!"

"Really?" When she nodded, he grinned. "I been prac-
ticin'."

"It shows." She really liked this kid. He was a redhead
like his mom and just a friendly, funny little boy.

"Thanks." He simply beamed. "Do you have to go?"

She stepped on the walkway leading to the porch and
the stairway up to her apartment. "Why?"

"Wanna see me do headers?"

If she was pregnant, spending a few minutes with this

child wouldn't change anything. And she really wasn't in that big a hurry to face the catastrophe that was her life.
"Header? Isn't that where you bounce the ball off your head?"

"Sort of."

"Doesn't that hurt?"

"Nah." He tossed the ball in the air a couple of times and tried to get under it, but misjudged. He was, after all, only seven.

"Good try, C.J."

"I'm not so good at that."

"You'll get the hang of it."

"I guess. Ya gotta sorta catch it with your head and kinda sorta use your body to get it down to your foot."

She smiled. "It sounds like you've been listening to your coach."

"My dad's been helpin' me."

Ellie knew he meant Adam Stone. She remembered the wedding and how proudly this child had said Adam was going to be his dad for real now and apparently he wasn't just talking the talk. He was walking the walk, too. The man had embraced this child as his own, and she thought that was awesome. At the same time she couldn't help wondering about Alex as a father.

At the wedding he'd told her about the woman who'd betrayed him and the son he'd thought was his. How he would always miss the boy. How would she feel if she was pregnant with his child? Betrayed yet again? Or happy to actually be a father?

"So you like Adam?" she asked.

C.J. stood in front of her, the ball under his arm. "I love him. But—"

"What?" There was a funny look on his face. "Is something wrong?"

He shrugged. "My mom and dad asked me if I want a baby brother or sister."

Apparently they were planning to start on those three siblings for this little boy. "How do you feel about that?"

"I guess it would be cool. But Mommy said a baby takes a lot of time. And I'd have to share."

So, they were talking about adding to the family and subtly planting the seed with their son. "But you'd have someone to play with. And your mom and dad will always love you. Y'all are the first and had the most time with your mom all by yourself."

He thought about that for a while, then grinned. "I'll be the biggest."

"Your brother or sister will look up to you."

"Yeah." He nodded. "I guess it will be pretty okay."

"I have three big brothers. They live in Texas and take good care of me." The Hart brothers might give her a hard time, but while they were around she'd never be alone.

"How's your broken leg?" C.J. asked. "Mommy said you couldn't climb up the stairs, so you had to move."

"That's right." As it turned out, the crisis happened before the move. A pregnancy would turn her life upside down, but living with Alex even for a short time could do a number on her heart.

"Is it all better?"

"It's fine. No more crutches."

"So you can play with me?"

"What did you have in mind?"

"I'll just kick the ball to you. Not hard. And you can do it back to me."

The truth was, she'd rather stand here and hang out with this funny little guy than go upstairs and face the music. "Okay. For a few minutes."

"Cool."

Ellie set her purse and bag on the bottom porch step, then turned. "Okay. I'm ready."

He stood several feet away and nudged the ball toward her. "Here it comes."

She kicked it back with her uninjured foot. "You've got a strong leg."

"That's what my dad says."

It was surprisingly relaxing listening to him chatter away while moving the ball back and forth. She could have kept it up longer, but she couldn't forget a rhyme her mother always repeated.

Procrastination is a crime. It only leads to sorrow. I can stop it anytime. I think I will tomorrow.

She kicked the ball back to C.J. "This has been fun, kiddo. But I really have to go."

Behind her, the front door opened and she heard Jill say, "C.J., you shouldn't be bothering Ellie."

"I wasn't, Mom. She wanted to play."

Ellie turned and smiled. "It's true."

The young woman looked doubtful as she walked out to the top step. "That's nice of you, but shouldn't you be off your feet? After all, you just got rid of the crutches."

"That would probably be wise." She glanced at the boy. "I gotta go in."

"O-okay." The disappointment in his voice was oddly heartwarming. Then his face brightened. "I'll show you my biggest, strongest kick."

"Make it a good one," Ellie encouraged.

He dropped the ball and backed away, then ran toward it and kicked as hard as he could. It passed Ellie and hit her things sitting on the bottom step. The bag fell sideways and one of the pregnancy test boxes fell out.

"Oh, no— I hope there's nothing breakable." Jill hurried down the steps and picked up the bag.

"It's fine. Don't worry. I—" Ellie moved at the same time and saw the other woman's eyes widen. There's no way she didn't see the pregnancy test.

"Sorry, Ellie. I guess I'm stronger than I thought." C.J. ran over and picked up the ball. He looked at what was in his mother's hands. "Hey, Mom, that looks just like the box you got."

Jill put it back in and handed the bag over. "I'm really not sure what to say."

"I guess congratulations are in order for you and Adam." Ellie wished the earth would open and swallow her whole. "And I'd appreciate it if you wouldn't say anything about this."

"Got it." The other woman nodded. "Are you happy about it?"

"'Bout what?" C.J. glanced first at his mother then at Ellie.

"That I'm off my crutches," Ellie answered, thinking fast.

"Mom, she already told me she's glad about that," the boy said.

"If you need anything— Or even to talk," Jill offered.

"Thanks. Now I really have to go upstairs. See you, C.J."

"Bye." He ran up the steps and into the house.

"Seriously, Ellie, if I can help, don't hesitate."

"I'll let you know," she said, trying to smile. "Bye."

She walked past the other woman and up the stairs, grateful to be alone. All of a sudden procrastination lost its appeal. It wasn't that she believed Jill would get on the phone tree and spread this around, but stuff didn't tend to stay secret in a small town like this. If she was actually pregnant, she needed to be the one to tell Alex.

Marching straight to the bathroom, she read the directions on the box several times to make sure of what to do. Morning would be the best time, but she couldn't wait that long. So she did what the instructions said.

It didn't take long for the result and when she saw, the moment was surreal.

"Oh, my God—"

The cell phone rang just as she was starting to freak out. It was Linc and she automatically answered. "Hello?"

"Hi, El. How are you?"

"Fine." That was such a lie, but she needed to pull herself together and process this information before breaking the news to her family. And it wasn't going to happen in a phone call. Harts didn't take the easy way out.

"So, are you on schedule?"

Not really, no, she wanted to say. But he was talking about her ankle. "The cast came off."

Since the day Linc had called while Alex was driving her around the lake, Ellie had managed to sidestep the questions about the man she worked with who'd driven her to the hospital and took care of her afterward. It had never been necessary to clue him in about her change in living arrangements, because he didn't know her rented apartment was a problem that Alex had fixed.

"How does it feel?"

"What?"

"To have the cast off." There was a note of impatience in his tone, as if he knew she was distracted.

"Fine." She needed to get off the phone. "I have to go—"

"Why?" There was an intensity in her brother's voice. "What's wrong?"

"Nothing."

"Not buying it, Ellie."

This was when how well he knew her was inconvenient. "Can't help that."

"There's something up with you."

"I have to go, Linc—"

"If you hang up on me again, I swear I'm coming down there."

"Up."

"What are you talking about?"

"Montana is north of Texas. Therefore it's up from Texas if one is looking at a map."

He took a long breath. "Tell me."

"You're imagining things. I'm completely fine." Physically fine, mentally she was a mess.

"And there it is again. That four-letter word meant to be reassuring but the more you say it, the less I believe."

"How suspicious can you get." It wasn't a question because she really didn't want to know. But Linc had a habit of telling her, anyway.

"Of course I'm suspicious." That confirmed the hunch that he planned to tell her. "You deliberately led me to believe it was a woman from work who was helping you when you first broke your ankle. Then the truth came out and you dodged my questions. Yeah, I noticed. And that tends to make a brother suspicious."

"Don't yell at me." She was starting to crack.

"I'm not." He sighed. "I'm concerned. You're my baby sister and I love you.

"I love you, too—"

When tears filled her eyes it was a bad time to get that yelling would have been better than his tender concern. Yelling would have given her an excuse for righteous indignation and she could have gotten mad. She looked at the positive pregnancy stick again and started to sniffle.

"Are you crying?"

"No—" But emotion choked off the rest of her words.

"Ellie Hart, tell me what the hell is going on with you?"

It was the worry in his voice that finally undid her. "I'm pregnant." For several long moments there was silence on the phone but she knew it wouldn't last. And it didn't.

"Ellie— Damn it. You just can't stay away from on-the-job complications, can you?"

"This is not a good time to tease me about my mistake."

"I'm not teasing. This is me being dead serious." And then the phone went dead.

In a world where it seemed as if everything was going wrong, something finally went right. At least she was in the bathroom when her stomach decided to turn on her.

Chapter Twelve

Ellie had been alone in the construction trailer the following day, and around quitting time she was about to go nuts waiting for Alex. Since seeing the positive pregnancy stick, she'd been trying to figure out a good way to break it to him. Something along the lines of "Good news. I'm pregnant." Or, "Remember that one time on the boat? Now I've got a baby on board." Or, "What do you think about becoming a father?"

She'd finally come to the conclusion there *was* no good way to tell him about this. Straight out was the best way. Like pulling off a Band-Aid—the quicker, the better. Then she'd follow that up with *It's a weird situation and needs to be figured out.* Now that she thought about it, also weird was that Linc hadn't called her back. But she couldn't worry about him right now.

"I can't sit in here, either." She stood and walked out from behind her desk toward the door. "I'm going crazy."

Outside she went down the three steps to the asphalt, past where her rental car was parked, and headed for the clinic addition. From here it looked really good, the exterior seamlessly attached to the old Victorian house donated by the founding family of Blackwater Lake to be used for medical purposes. She'd taken great care when designing the elevation to make sure the graceful lines and architectural style of the original structure were incorporated into the new section so it wouldn't look like an afterthought, just tacked on.

She walked inside where a crew was installing cupboards in exam rooms and baseboards throughout. There was a faint smell of sawdust, not as strong as during the framing phase, but still pleasant. There was something so clean, fresh and promising about wood being cut and formed in the beginning stages of a new venture.

Sinks, countertops, paint and flooring were on the schedule to be installed. It was all but finished and, professionally speaking, everything had gone smoothly. Personally, not so much.

"Hey, Ellie."

Standing where the new section connected with the old in the reception area, she turned at the sound of the deep voice. It was a lot like Alex's but not. Ben McKnight stood there in the empty waiting room just a few feet from the sliding-glass window where the receptionist sat and greeted patients. He'd just come down the stairs from his office on the second floor.

"Hi, Doc." She smiled in greeting. "Are y'all finished for the day?"

He nodded. "This was supposed to be a half day."

"To golf?"

"That's a cliché. And I don't particularly like golf. Not

good at it." He smiled. "But we schedule light one day a week and try to get home to our families."

She looked at the watch on her wrist. "Not so much today."

"Had an emergency. Skateboard accident. Broken arm."

"I'm sorry to hear that. Is he doing okay?"

"What makes you think the patient was a boy?"

"I have brothers. They were in the emergency room so often my mother knew the names of everyone on staff and their families." She shrugged.

"And you're right." He grinned. "The patient is a boy who decided to do a flip off the curb, and his arm didn't take the landing well. Speaking of that, how's the ankle feel?"

"It aches a little when I'm on my feet for a while, and can we talk about the peeling skin?" She wrinkled her nose. "Gross."

He laughed. "That's normal. Exfoliate gently. I promise it won't last long."

"Good to know I won't be shedding forever." Looking up at the ceiling where the old and new came together, she asked, "So, what do y'all think of the place?"

"Looks really good. Can't wait to spread out and expand services." He slid his hands into the pockets of the white lab coat he still wore. "We're starting the search for another doctor to join the clinic staff."

Interesting about more staff. This was a small town. Her brother had called it "Black Hole." He'd been teasing, but it didn't have the lure of a big city. In her opinion, there was a lot to be said for living here; the place had grown on her. But some people, especially after the education and training required to practice medicine, might decide it wasn't enough for them. People like Alex's ex-wife, who'd let him believe for a while that he had everything, then decided she had nothing in this small town.

"How hard do you think it will be to find someone?" she asked.

"It could take a while," Ben admitted.

"I hope it's not long. This is a wonderful place. Anyone would be lucky to live here."

"It's not very big." He was echoing her own thoughts. "Major shopping and entertainment aren't right around the corner."

"The really important things don't require traveling," she argued. "Friendly people who go out of their way to make a stranger feel welcome. Neighbors who pitch in when someone needs help. It has the lake. And mountains. This is a place where a family can bond and children learn values and the importance of community in their lives."

One of his dark eyebrows lifted. "If I didn't know better, I'd say you don't want to leave."

"There are projects waiting for me in Dallas." That didn't really answer the question, but she couldn't. Alex seemed perfectly willing to let her go based on how easily he'd watched her move out of his house.

"It seems to me that you and my brother work together pretty well."

"Did you think we wouldn't?" Funny that he mentioned Alex, as if he'd been reading her mind.

"Not really." He frowned. "I just remember when he was inspecting the house he was building for me and he mentioned a meeting with you."

"Oh?" That was noncommittal, but she desperately wanted to hear if he'd said something nice. Or not nice. But this was the real world, not junior high school.

"Yeah. I said something and he bit my head off." He

folded his arms over his chest. "Do you have any idea what's been bugging him lately?"

That surprised her. The only difference she'd noticed in him since she'd moved back to her apartment was a retreat to friendly but impersonal. It was the way he'd acted when she'd first arrived on the job site. She couldn't fault him, though. He'd never promised more than having fun. But he made it seem so easy to forget her.

"Why do you think there's something wrong?"

"He was here first thing this morning. Usually I'm not, but I had to do some paperwork."

"What happened?"

"Your name came up."

Her heart started to pound. "Really?"

"I was telling him about the city council meeting last night. The mayor mentioned having an open house for the clinic. Giving tours of the new facility to generate publicity and announce expanded services."

"And Alex was angry about that?"

"Not until I said that it would be nice if you were here for that." He shrugged in a way that said he didn't understand the reaction. "Although my brother would be happy to take all the congratulations on a job well done, he couldn't have done the project without you."

"I appreciate that very much, Ben."

Those words were appropriate, which was a miracle considering she was wondering why Alex would be angry at his brother for mentioning her. Probably it would violate the fun-until-you-leave pact. There was no clause about her coming back for a grand opening or anything more personal than that.

She forced herself to smile. "I hope that means I can count on a positive recommendation from Blackwater

Lake when I submit plans and bid for my next freelance job. I'm going to put Mercy Medical Clinic on my résumé."

"I think I speak for the whole town when I say you can count on everyone singing your praises."

"Good." Suddenly, she just wanted to be by herself. Apparently the stress of having to tell Alex he was going to be a father had taken a lot out of her. She didn't have the reserves for small talk, especially with his brother. "Okay, then. It was good to see you. But I have to go."

Ben looked concerned. "Are you all right, Ellie?"

"Yes. Why?"

"You look tired."

There was a reason for that and he would find out soon enough, but his brother needed to know first. "I'm fine."

He nodded thoughtfully. "A broken bone seems like an isolated trauma, but it affects your whole body. Healing can take a lot out of you. It's okay to rest, especially now that the pressure of the clinic expansion is easing."

He was very kind, and it bothered her that she couldn't tell him the reason for her fatigue. That would be up to Alex. And where the heck was he? If he didn't show up soon, she'd call him when she got back to her apartment and arrange to meet somewhere.

"I'll remember to take it easy. Thanks for the advice, Ben."

He nodded. "If you have discomfort or pain, get it checked out."

In Dallas was what he meant. "Count on it. I better be going."

"Me, too. I'm taking Cam out to dinner."

"Have you two set a date yet for the wedding?" she asked him.

"We're nailing it down," he said mysteriously. "Can't be soon enough for me."

"Have fun tonight."

"We always do." Turning away, he started to whistle as he shrugged out of his lab coat.

Ellie envied them. Camille Halliday was a lucky woman, and the newly engaged couple were expecting a baby. Ben was a happy man, so it would seem that he didn't mind becoming a father. Maybe it was in the DNA and Alex could be okay with it, too.

She walked outside, her gaze automatically drawn to the construction trailer. Alex's black truck was there and he was just getting out. Her stomach dropped; this was the moment of truth. Face-to-face, the way any child of Hastings Hart would handle the situation. There was no way to control Alex's reaction. It would be what it would be, and she wished there was a way to spare him this news, but he had to know.

Ellie blew out a long breath and started toward him. When she'd covered half the distance, a car came screeching into the lot. That was noteworthy, since it was past quitting time. But when she looked more closely, she saw that it was a rental from the airport where she'd gotten hers. A tall, familiar-looking, dark-haired man got out and her stomach dropped again. For a different reason.

"Oh, my God. No. Linc—"

There was only one reason her brother would be here.

She started to run, but the muscles in her left leg were still weak and wouldn't let her. It was frustrating not to be able to move faster, when she saw her brother stop in front of Alex. Finally she was only a few feet away, near enough to hear Linc say, "Are you Alex McKnight?"

"Yes. What can I do for you—"

Without warning Linc's fist shot out and caught Alex on the cheek, snapping his head back.

"That's for getting my sister pregnant."

Ellie stepped between the two men who both towered over her. She was facing her brother and the forward momentum of his body convinced her he planned to hit Alex again.

"Stop it, Linc."

"Get out of the way, Ellie." Her brother's blue eyes blazed with fury. "No one takes advantage of my little sister and gets away with it."

"That's not what happened." She glanced over her shoulder at Alex, who looked equally furious and ready to retaliate for the sucker punch. Someone was going to get hurt unless they cooled down, and she cared very much about both of these men. She looked at her brother. "For pity's sake, calm down."

"Not yet." He put his hands on her arms and tried to move her.

"Don't be ridiculous." She refused to let him budge her. "There are laws against assaulting someone on the street. Y'all will get arrested."

"In Black Hole, Montana? I don't think so." Linc's voice dripped sarcasm.

She could almost feel the waves of fury rolling off Alex and turned to him. "He didn't mean that."

"Yes, I did."

Alex's mouth tightened. "In Montana, we introduce ourselves before throwing a punch."

"Name's Lincoln Hart, and you're going to regret the day you used my sister."

"It wasn't like that," she protested. When Alex took a step forward, she put her hands on his chest to stop him. "Don't, Alex. Please."

"Let him go, Ellie. I don't need my sister to protect me. I can take care of myself."

"No, you can't, Linc." Furiously she turned back to her

brother. "He carries stacks of two-by-fours as if they were toothpicks. You sit behind a desk and talk on the phone."

"Now just a damn minute—"

"No. You listen to me." She stared him down. "It's a smartphone, but hey, not the same. He could hurt you and I wouldn't blame him a bit. You're making an ass of yourself."

"I'm protecting your honor." He glared at her. "Let me at him. Now it's really personal."

"I'm not moving. You'll have to get through me and if you try it, you could hurt the baby." She watched that sink into her brother's head. "This is my problem. And I will deal with it as I see fit."

"But Ellie, I—"

"Not another word." She held up a finger to silence him.

"Really? This is the thanks I get?"

She fished keys out of her purse and took off the one that would unlock the front door of her apartment. "I live on Lake View Road. I suggest you stop and ask directions. Anyone in town will tell you how to get there. You'll stay with me."

"Isn't there a hotel in this town?"

"Blackwater Lake Lodge. But I wouldn't count on there being a vacancy." Not when she'd needed it, anyway. "Besides, I'd like you to stay at my place so I can keep an eye on you."

Behind her she heard the truck door open, then close. The engine roared to life, then it backed up and peeled out of the parking lot.

"I suggest you wait for me at my place, Linc. I also suggest you cool off."

"And if I don't?"

"The lake is a short walk. You might want to take a quick dip. It's really cold."

Rebellion flashed in his eyes as he dragged a hand through his light brown hair. "Where are you going?"

"To talk to Alex."

"Then you and I are going to talk," her brother warned.

"We always do." She started to turn away, then walked into his arms for a hug. "Your timing could have been better, but thanks for coming, Linc."

He wrapped her in his arms. "Anytime."

What was she going to say to Alex?

To think she'd spent the past twenty-four hours agonizing over how to tell him he was going to be a father. It never occurred to her that he'd find out in the worst possible way.

"Were you ever going to tell me you're pregnant?" Alex's voice was full of the betrayal still glittering in his eyes.

Forty minutes after he'd left the construction lot Ellie handed him a bag of frozen peas she'd just grabbed from his freezer. She'd guessed he would head for home, although she'd taken a drive past the local bar first and didn't see his truck. Texas girls were tough, but the two men were like a scene from *Clash of the Titans*. The only thing she could think of to stop them was playing the pregnant card. Fortunately it had worked, and now she was at his house to explain.

"Of course I was going to tell you," she finally answered.

"But you mentioned it to your brother first." Accusation joined the betrayal on his face and sharpened his features.

"Linc caught me at a weak moment. I was looking at a stick that said 'pregnant.' So sue me for saying something when I was upset."

This was exactly what she'd been afraid of. His ex-wife

had withheld vital information, like the fact that he wasn't her baby's father, and Alex had married her, moved the family to Blackwater Lake. Ellie could see where he would be sensitive about this.

She sat beside him on the family room sofa, the place where he'd made sure she elevated her broken ankle. She badly wanted to touch him, but couldn't risk it now.

"I don't need you to fight my battles."

"That's not what I was doing. It was my brother I was concerned about." She thought she'd made that clear. "My goal was to prevent bloodshed, but apparently I trampled all over male pride."

"It's not about that. He had it all wrong."

"And he was in no mood to hear the truth. I'll make everything clear when I see him." Hopefully that would put an end to that. She set her purse on the sofa beside her. "Alex, just so we're clear, the baby is yours."

"I never thought it wasn't."

"Yes, you did. Maybe just for a second, but I understand why." She looked at the bright red mark on his cheek that was beginning to swell and turn dark. "Put the bag on your face. That will help."

"Will it?"

She nodded. "Y'all will probably have a shiner, anyway, but maybe not as bad if you put cold on it now."

"If only it was good for more than black eyes." He tossed the bag on the coffee table.

Okay, Ellie thought, now he was being childish and stubborn. She was over cutting him slack and taking the heat for another woman's sin. She was pregnant and didn't get this way by herself.

"Look, I'm only going to say this one more time, so listen up, mister. I just did the test yesterday, and Linc happened to call while I was trying to take it all in. I wasn't keeping it a secret from you. This is information I didn't think you should hear over the phone. My plan was to tell you face-to-face at work today, but you weren't there." Until, as fate would have it, her brother showed up. The expression on his face hadn't changed and that made her madder. "So now you know the God's-honest truth. I take my fair share of blame for this situation, but it was your responsibility to buy foolproof condoms."

"There's no such thing."

"Then we both share fault." She stood and started for the door. "That's all I have to say. My work here is done."

"Just a minute—"

"No. My brother's waiting."

"This is more important than Rocky Balboa cooling his fists for a while."

"I'm not so sure," she said. "He's my support system."

"And you're carrying my baby."

Ellie turned to look at him. There was still tension in every line and angle of his face, but the suspicious expression was gone. "I didn't plan for any of this to happen."

"I know."

"Okay." She nodded. "So, I think we should let the information sink in and then we'll come up with a plan of action."

"There's nothing to sink in. We're going to be parents. And there's only one thing to do."

"What?"

"I'll marry you as soon as possible."

I'll marry you. Not—we should get married. The phrasing spoke volumes.

She could see he was completely serious and really, why was she so surprised? Martha had said Alex would do the right thing. It's just that Ellie had thought the housekeeper had meant in a financial way and having a relationship with his child. Not a shotgun wedding.

"Aren't you going to say something?" he asked.

"I'm not sure what to say."

He stood and never looked away. He never moved closer, either. "How about yes?"

Ellie had been badly burned in her last relationship, and she swore she wouldn't be so stupid again. But occasionally she'd let her guard down and let herself just think about a marriage proposal. It had always included a passionate declaration of love before the M word. And because she hadn't heard that, the hurt she felt now was so much worse than finding out she'd been made a fool of.

It was ironic, really, that she could so clearly see he didn't have deep, romantic feelings for her. It was that exact moment she realized without a doubt she was in love with him.

And so she had an answer to the question. "I can't marry you."

"Why the hell not?"

"Because y'all are just being noble."

"And that's a bad thing?" He dragged his fingers through his hair.

"No. It's an admirable quality. But if marriage isn't right for you and me it would be wrong for the baby."

"Who says it isn't right?" he demanded. "We're friends. I like you. You like me. We're good together in bed."

All of that was too true, except the part about her liking him. It was so much more than that. "I appreciate the offer. You're a good man. But—"

"What?" He stood straight, clearly bracing himself for the answer.

"I want a husband and partner. A relationship. Not a McKnight in shining armor."

"That's not what this is. We're having a baby, and that child deserves a family."

"*Family* has many definitions besides marriage. And you don't need to do me any favors." She picked up her purse and pointed to the bag of frozen peas on the table. "Put that on your face."

Before he could say more, Ellie walked away. It wasn't so much that she didn't want to listen, but there were tears in her eyes and she wouldn't let him see. Marriage was a good offer, but she wanted more.

She wanted Alex McKnight to love her.

Chapter Thirteen

The next day Alex was in a foul mood when he got home from work, even fouler than it had been when Ellie moved out of his house. He walked in the kitchen where Martha was cutting up vegetables and made a conscious decision not to take it out on her.

"What's for dinner?" His tone was very pleasant, he thought, considering how close he was to putting his fist through a wall.

Knife in hand, she glanced up at him. "Chicken piccata."

It was Ellie's favorite, and the fact that he knew put his bad mood on turboboost. "You do know I'm not crazy about that?"

"But Ellie is."

"She's not here."

"Okay. I can put this away for tomorrow if you're taking her out to dinner." She reached into the cupboard for a plastic storage container.

"There's not going to be a dinner out," he informed her.

Martha turned, and there was a disapproving expression on her face. "Why not?"

"Why would I?"

"Because the two of you have things to talk about, what with her having your baby."

"How the hell do you know that?" he demanded.

"I work here." The look on her face said, *Duh.* "I know things."

Of course she did, but apparently not quite everything. "She's gone."

"Tell me something I don't know. She moved back to her apartment. I helped her pack."

"No." The emptiness in his gut got a little bigger, a lot deeper. "She left town."

"I didn't hear that." The housekeeper's eyes showed her surprise, but there was no satisfaction in scooping her. "How do you know?"

"Adam Stone told me. Her brother took her home to Texas, and she dropped the key to her apartment off with Jill before they left. She said her work at the clinic was done."

Alex knew there was some truth in that but figured more likely she was done with him.

"So, what are you going to do about her?" Martha put her fists on her hips and waited for his answer.

"This isn't about her."

"Oh?"

"She's just another woman who ran out. But she's carrying my child. *That's* what this is about. The relevant question would be what am I going to do about the baby."

Her mouth pulled tight for a moment. "Nice shiner. I hear her brother gave it to you."

"Just once could something happen in this town that everyone doesn't know about?"

"Next time you might want to take the fight inside where the construction crew doesn't have a front-row seat."

He glared at her. "It was a lucky punch. And he was dead wrong about the situation."

"So you're not the guy who got his sister pregnant?"

"Not on purpose." Damn that ancient condom. And Ellie had been an eager participant. She'd wanted him as much as he'd wanted her. Hell, he still wanted her, which made no sense since she left without a word to him. "It just happened."

"When you play the game, you have to be ready to accept the consequences."

"Who are you? My mother?"

"I'm as close as you've got," she snapped back. "Can you blame her brother for defending his sister? If some Romeo got Sydney pregnant, what would you do?"

He admitted, if only to himself, that she had a point. "Let my brother, Ben, deck him," he said angrily.

"Ben's a doctor—a surgeon. Can't take a chance with his hands."

"What about mine? I work for a living."

"Not with a hammer anymore." Martha folded her arms over her chest as her gaze narrowed accusingly. "What did you do to Ellie? Besides get her pregnant, I mean."

"What makes you think *I* did something?"

She shrugged. "Educated guess. That girl fit in here in Blackwater Lake. She loves this place like she'd been born to it. She left in an awful big hurry, and my gut's telling me she had a good reason. The only good reason I can think of has to involve you."

"Don't see how. I did the right thing. I asked her to marry me."

Interest sparkled in her eyes. "What did she say?"

"That I was just being noble."

"Ah."

He was pretty sure that didn't sound good. "What does that mean?"

"It's for you to figure out."

Definitely not good, he thought. "Since when am I the bad guy? You do know I sign your paycheck, right?"

"Oh, please…" The glance she gave him was all kinds of pitying. "You can't get along without me."

"No one is indispensable."

"That's where you're wrong. Ellie is a good woman, with a good heart."

What the hell did that mean? Martha Spooner never had good things to say about the women he saw. And she'd had a lot to say about his ex-wife, none of it good.

"Who are you and what have you done with my house-keeper?"

"I have no idea what you mean."

"Ellie left *me*. Shouldn't you be on my side?"

"I say again—she had a good reason."

"Why are you sticking up for her? You never did for Laurel."

"Mrs. McKnight." She sniffed as if there was suddenly a bad smell in the room. "That witch was wrong for you."

He'd expected her to say the woman he'd married was a liar who'd used him then cheated in a different way with the guy who'd fathered her baby. Now Alex was going to be a father, and Martha was siding with the woman carrying his child.

The question had to be asked. "So you think Ellie is right for me?"

"I didn't say that."

"Okay, this is me asking if you think she is."

Martha held up her hands. "Don't drag me into this."

"Since when do you not have an opinion?"

"Since now. Only you can decide who is or isn't right for you." She put the plastic container of chicken in the refrigerator then walked out of the room.

This thing with Ellie wasn't supposed to get complicated, Alex thought. It was just having fun. A fling. By definition that meant short-term, and when she left no one would get hurt. They'd go back to their regularly scheduled lives she'd said. But he experienced the flaw in the plan when she'd moved back to her apartment. Missing her so much he ached from it had taken him completely by surprise.

The first time he'd reached for her in his bed and came up empty he got angry, then just felt empty. The same thing happened every time he walked into a room in this house expecting to see her and she wasn't there. Deep inside he knew this place would never be the same without her in it. The devil was that he had no idea how to make everything go back to the way it was.

And now she was pregnant, and there was no doubt in his mind that he was the baby's father. Part of him was happy to have another chance, but mostly he was ticked off that she'd left town. No, there was nothing easy about this at all. And he was definitely not having fun.

Martha came back in the room and said, "Bye, Alex. I'll see you tomorrow."

"No, you won't. Ellie and I have some things to work out."

"And how are you going to do that?"

"I'm catching a plane to Dallas."

The smile on his housekeeper's face was pure approval. "That's the spirit."

* * *

Ellie loved her parents' home in an affluent suburb of Dallas. She'd loved growing up here with the dark-wood floors, serene earth-tone walls and crown molding on the high ceilings. The sofas were plush, and the dining room table could easily hold thirty people for a dinner party.

Her childhood bedroom upstairs had its own bath and a queen-size canopy bed with ruffled bedskirt and pink comforter. There were enough shams and throw pillows to choke a Texas-size herd of longhorns. In Blackwater Lake, seeing and talking to her brother had made it seem incredibly important to go back home, but now she wasn't so sure. She hurt deep inside from wanting to see Alex, to be with him. He had her cell number and knew where to find her, but so far there wasn't a word from him.

Hastings and Katherine Hart knew they were going to be grandparents. Linc would have told them, anyway, so she'd broken the news the day before yesterday, as soon as she'd seen them after coming home from Blackwater Lake. Thirty years ago her mother had quite a promising acting career before she'd married then immediately became pregnant with Ellie's oldest brother. But performance art must have been instinctive to her, because it was impossible to tell whether the woman felt happy, excited or disappointed at the prospect of becoming a grandmother. And her father must have caught the performance bug from his wife, because he was also impossible to read.

They'd just finished dinner, and the three of them were having coffee in the family room. Well, her parents had china saucers and cups filled with the dark, rich-smelling stuff, but not so much for Ellie. She'd seen an obstetrician—the Harts knew people, including doctors, and had pulled strings to get her right in—and he'd recommended against it. As much as she liked her coffee, she felt it wasn't wise to ignore the professional advice. But when Ina Wheeler, the Harts' longtime housekeeper, had brought her a bowl of mixed fruit while Hasty and Kate had chocolate cake and ice cream, she'd been a little crabby.

"How are the strawberries, Suellen?" her mother asked.

"Yummy." She glared at one, then stabbed it with her silver fork and popped it into her mouth.

"It's so good to have you home." Kate took a delicate bite of cake, then put down her fork and wiped her mouth on the cloth napkin.

Her mother was in her late fifties but looked twenty years younger. A lot of people thought she was Ellie's sister—they were of identical height, and both had deep blue eyes and the same hair color, light brown with highlights. Of course they both went to the same exclusive Dallas salon. Kate's hair was razor-cut in an edgy bob while Ellie preferred longer layers.

"Your mother is right. We've missed you."

Her father had finished his dessert and set the empty plate on the dark-wood coffee table where Ina almost instantly whisked it away. He was in his early sixties, with pale blue eyes and gray hair. His wife said it only made him more distinguished. Theirs had been a love affair since the moment they met, but Ellie had never understood giving up a profitable career to marry and have children.

Now her perspective was different. She was pregnant, and single. There was no choice for her about working. She planned to support herself and her child. She'd only ever wanted her family to be as proud of her as she was of them, and sponging off the folks wasn't the way to do that.

There were two wing chairs facing the fireplace, with love seats flanking them. Her parents were side by side in the chairs and her father crossed one leg over the other.

"Your mother and I have been talking, and we think it would be a good idea for you to stay here with us."

Ellie had been there since returning from Blackwater Lake, but that morning she had mentioned her intention to return to her condo close to the Hart Industries building in downtown Dallas. "You mean just one more night?"

"Actually we thought it could be a permanent arrangement." Her mother stirred sugar into her coffee. "Think how lovely it would be to turn the bedroom next to yours into a nursery."

"You don't want to deal with a crying baby." The gesture made her emotional, but she couldn't afford to go soft right now. Hopefully they would grab the excuse she was handing them on a silver platter and let this go.

"Have you seen the size of this house?" her father joked. "You're in the other wing. We won't hear a thing."

"You'd have your privacy and also support with the baby. If necessary," her mother added.

"It's a very generous offer. I'll think about it."

"That means no." Kate's tone was matter-of-fact, without anger or judgment.

"Why would you go there from what I said?"

"Because I study people and body language. That habit goes back to my time on the stage. I'm also your mother and I know you better than anyone. Since you were a little girl, if there was something you didn't want to do that's what you'd say. Very passive-aggressive, by the way."

And a good coping skill in order to avoid a knock-down, drag-out fight. She was impressed that her mom had noticed. Did one need acting skills to be so observant, or was it a mom thing? Ellie hoped she would know her own baby that well.

She smiled at them. "I'm not avoiding the issue, but it really is a big decision."

"I understand." Kate looked at her husband. "But I'm sure your father doesn't."

"Hell, no, I don't understand." He set his cup and saucer on the table. "I just want to protect my little girl."

Parental protective instincts were something she was starting to get. When the OB doctor had said that everything looked normal and fine with the baby, she'd been very relieved.

"You still look tired, Suellen. At least stay here with us a little longer so you can get some rest. We can make sure you eat right, too," her mother said. "And I don't want to hear that you'll think about it."

"I really should get back to my place. But I very much appreciate the offer."

The sooner she got into a routine that didn't include Alex, the better off she'd be. And maybe she was punishing herself for yet another personal mistake. The penance was doing this on her own; the reward would be confidence and self-respect. That was very important to her and the whole reason she'd taken the job in Blackwater Lake to begin with.

Before her parents could try to change her mind, the doorbell rang and Ina called from the kitchen, "I'll get it."

Her father looked at his watch. "I wonder if that's one of the boys."

The boys being her brothers—Linc, Cal and Sam, from youngest to oldest. "Since when would they ring the bell? Don't they just walk in?"

"Yes," her mother agreed. "And it's a little late for anyone to come calling."

The housekeeper in her gray dress with the white apron was very different from Martha Spooner, who wore jeans to work. When she came back into the room, she announced there was a man there to see Ellie.

"Did he give his name?" her dad asked.

"Alex McKnight."

"The baby's father," his wife said. She didn't look happy.

Hastings stood. "I've got a thing or two to say to him."

Ellie's heart started pounding so hard it almost hurt. The expression on her father's face was a lot like the one Linc had worn before throwing that punch.

Ellie stood, too. "Don't you hit him, Dad."

"I didn't plan to. Your brother already took care of that."

She wasn't reassured. "I want to speak to him alone. This is my problem and I'll handle it."

Her parents studied her for several moments then her mother nodded. "We'll be right upstairs, and Ina is in the kitchen if you need any help."

"It will be fine," she lied. The kind of help she needed they couldn't give her.

Then the three of them walked into the spacious entryway with twin curving staircases where Alex waited. The sight of him went straight to Ellie's soul and filled it up. He was wearing slacks and a matching jacket with a light blue dress shirt unbuttoned at the neck.

It was a good look, but she missed the jeans, T-shirt and work boots. He was also wearing a still-colorful bruise on his cheek, the mark proving that her honor had been defended. Probably her father wouldn't approve if she walked over and caressed that shiner the way she wanted.

"Hello, Alex." She moved closer. "These are my parents—Hastings and Katherine Hart. This is Alex McKnight."

"It's a pleasure to meet you Mr. Hart, Mrs. Hart." He held out his hand, but neither accepted the peace offering and he let it fall to his side. His mouth pulled tight for a moment before he said, "I've come to see Ellie."

"We know." Her father's voice held barely controlled fury.

The sooner she got him alone, the better. "Mom and Dad were just going upstairs."

"Not voluntarily," her father said.

"Come along, Hasty." Her mother took his hand and without another word the two of them went up the left staircase leading to the second floor.

"We can go into the family room," Ellie said.

The house was big but she knew that if you stood in the right spot upstairs, conversations could be overheard. Ellie heard his steps behind her and she desperately wanted to take his hand the way her mother had done with her father, but she didn't have the right. A proposal without love didn't change what she and Alex had, which was nothing. The fling was over. He was only here because of the baby. The fact that he was here was something, anyway.

Alex stopped in front of the fireplace and looked around. "This is quite a place."

"Yeah. It's where I grew up." She couldn't stare at his face hard enough. "How's the eye?"

"Looks worse than it is."

"Has anyone noticed?"

"Are you kidding? In Blackwater Lake?" His expression was wry, then all amusement disappeared and accusation took its place. "You ran out on the Mercy Medical Clinic job."

"Not true. My part in the project was finished." She didn't add that for the past week or so she'd been making up reasons to hang around. It was only a few days ago that she'd realized she'd been doing it because she was in love with him.

His mouth pulled into a tight, tense line. "Then it was

me you were running out on. At least my ex made an announcement before she left."

He was right, but the words stung. He was lumping her in the same category as the woman who'd used and lied to him. "I had my reasons."

"And I have rights."

"You mean the baby." She was standing in front of him, near enough to feel the heat from his body, close enough for him to fold her into his arms. "You should know that I saw the doctor yesterday. Everything is fine. I told him about my ankle and the surgery but he was certain there wouldn't be any problem. The small amount of anesthesia won't affect the baby. They took blood and I'll be seeing him on a regular basis."

"I'm glad to hear it."

"Just so you know, my lawyer will be in touch. We'll come up with a custody arrangement and generous visitation rights. I'd never keep you from your child."

"I never thought you would."

"The thing is, I have to work, and my contacts are tied up with Hart Industries here in Dallas." She loved her job and was willing to juggle it with motherhood regardless of the circumstances. If he loved her, they could come up with a strategy together, but that wasn't the case. It was her sole responsibility to plot the course of her career and figure out how to do that and be a mother.

"I understand."

"So, if that's it, I'll see you out."

He held up his hand. "Not so fast."

"What else is there to say?"

"You need to know that I'm planning to open a branch of McKnight Construction here in Dallas."

"You would do that? Why?"

"To make things easier on you and the baby." He

dragged his fingers through his hair, clearly not as cool as he pretended. "This is my child, too. I lost a little boy I thought was mine, and that's the worst. It's not going to happen again. I want to be there for everything. The doctor's appointments, the birth. Everything."

She wished with all her heart that the magnanimous gesture was about her and not simply his guaranteeing that he would see their child. She was only included because she was carrying the baby. If only things could be different. If only he could trust and love her. But that ship had sailed, and there was nothing to be done about it.

How in the world was she going to see him, share a child with him and all the contact that implied, and not let on that she loved him and wanted more?

"Okay, then," she said. "There's nothing else to talk about."

"There is," he said. "I still think we should get married."

"My answer is still the same. For the same reason. If you came to Dallas to get my family on your side, you should know it won't work."

He rubbed a knuckle across his cheek, just below the black-and-blue mark. "Your brother had a way of indicating whose side he was on, and it didn't include words."

"I have two more brothers."

"I know," he said. "And I have more to say. But not tonight. You look tired."

"I'm fine." That was a lie, because she'd never been more exhausted in her life. Fatigue made her feel vulnerable when she had to be strong. "I guess you're going back to Montana tomorrow."

"No. I'll be around for a while."

So much for establishing a routine without him in it. That just wasn't fair. "I'll see you out."

"Okay."

She didn't say anything, just walked him to the door and opened it. He hesitated a moment and it seemed as if he was going to kiss her, but he shook his head. "Good night, Ellie."

"Bye, Alex."

When he was gone, she leaned back against the door as her parents came down the stairs.

"What did he say?" her father demanded. "Is he going to do right by you?"

"He wants to be part of the baby's life." Which she now realized meant that he would always be part of hers, too. And the support her parents had offered before now seemed incredibly important. "Can I spend the night here with you guys?"

"As long as you want, sweetheart." Her mother hugged her.

"You have to protect me from him."

"I thought you said he's manned up and doing the honorable thing." Her father looked confused.

"He is. But I'm spineless around him and I'm counting on you guys to keep him away so I don't make a fool of myself."

Chapter Fourteen

She'd made him feel something again and he hated it.

Alex wouldn't be shut out of his child's life. This trip could have waited, except he wouldn't let it. Because Ellie had made him feel. Now she could slice and dice him with one of her sky-high stilettos and there wasn't much he could do to stop it.

He parked his rental car outside the Hart Industries building in downtown Dallas. It was all glass, chrome and angles.

"All Texas flash and dazzle," he muttered.

He definitely wasn't in Montana anymore. Except for the multistory buildings, the Lone Star State was flat as far as the eye could see. This flashy Hart headquarters was where all three of Ellie's siblings worked—Sam, Cal and Linc—each of them in a different business under the family umbrella. He'd seen more than one sign warning not to mess with Texas, and he had a hunch that wasn't just about litter.

Alex had no idea what he was going to say to Ellie's brothers, but his gut was telling him this was the right thing to do. He had a sister, and he hoped if she ever got pregnant, the guy would man up and face him. So, that was what he was doing. Linc already had his shot, but there was a good chance the other two would want theirs.

He pushed open the glass door and walked into the lobby. Looking around he said, "Impressive."

The marble floors, wood, plants, art and glass were all upscale and expensive. That meant anyone doing business here had more than a buck or two to spend. Hart Industries' clients would have a lot of zeroes in their bank accounts.

There was a pretty redhead sitting behind a mahogany desk. "May I help you?"

"I hope so—" he looked at the nameplate in front of her that said Bridget Quinlan "—Bridget. I'm here to see Mr. Hart."

"Which one?"

"All of them."

Her green eyes widened slightly. "I don't think that's going to be possible."

"Yeah, it is."

"Do you have an appointment?"

"No."

"I'd be happy to make one for you," she offered.

"If it's all the same to you, I'd like to get this over with today." He brushed his suit jacket aside and slid his hands into the pockets of his slacks. "They'll want to talk to me. Tell them Alex McKnight is here."

"All right." It took her a nanosecond to size him up and come to the conclusion he wasn't leaving until she did as requested. But her tone clearly said he was wasting his time. She picked up the phone. "Hi, Wendy. Can you tell them that there's a Mr. Alex McKnight here?" Seconds later she said, "Oh. Okay. Right away."

He couldn't miss the surprise in her voice and it was a big clue that he'd been right. "I guess that was the all clear."

"It was. Top floor. They're waiting for you."

"Thanks, Bridget."

"You're welcome." She watched him start to turn. "Mr. McKnight?"

"Yes?"

"Nice shiner."

"Thanks." Her way of telling him she knew this wasn't about business. "There's a better than even chance I'll have another one to match when I come back this way."

"Good luck."

"I'm going to need it."

He headed for the bank of elevators behind her and pushed the up button. When the doors opened, he got in and hit the one for the twelfth floor. Tension coiled in his gut for a lot of reasons, but at the moment he was focusing on self-defense. Linc had sucker-punched him, and he figured the other two Hart brothers each had one shot coming. If they wanted more, he'd make them work for it before security could get there and throw him out.

When the elevator doors opened, three men were standing there, all of them over six feet tall, and somehow he knew they were lined up in order of age. Behind them was a reception desk where Wendy was sitting, guarding access to the Harts. There was an expensive area rug with plush sofa and chairs. More plants and art made it an elegant place to wait for a meeting. And the three doorways off the open area were not a coincidence. At the end of each corridor was probably an office for a different branch of Hart industries.

He looked back at the men. It might have been a function of being badly outnumbered, but the thought crossed his mind that everything really was big in Texas. Like himself, each of them wore slacks, a white dress shirt and an expensive silk tie, nothing that would be friendly to blood splatter. They were waiting and he'd fire the first salvo.

"I'm Alex McKnight." After admitting who he was to Linc, offering his hand had been the biggest mistake. He didn't make the same one now. He nodded at the other man.

"I'm Sam Hart." The tallest brother spoke. Ellie had told him this was the oldest. Unlike his siblings, he had dark brown hair and eyes.

Process of elimination told him the man in the middle was Cal. His hair was light brown and his eyes pale blue. There was a definite family resemblance, basically the same shape face and slight differences in their eyes and mouths. They could all be models on the cover of a men's magazine with their identical square jaws, too.

"What do you want?" Sam asked.

"It's about Ellie and—"

"You got her pregnant." Cal's voice was deep and deadly.

Alex figured it would be counterproductive to explain their sister had been a willing participant during conception. He simply stated the obvious: "She's carrying my child."

"You took advantage of her," Linc accused.

"Did she tell you that?"

Cal didn't give his brother a chance to answer. "Ellie has a bad habit of trusting men she shouldn't."

"I'm not one of them."

"Right." Sam's voice dripped with skepticism.

"Look, you don't know me from a rock and have no reason to accept as true anything I say. In your place I'd probably do the same thing." The good news was they were still letting him talk. "The thing is, I'm here for her. And the baby," he added. "Nothing is going to change that."

"There's only one thing to do," Linc muttered. "You have to marry her."

Sam glanced at his younger brother, then back. "Why should we believe you'll keep showing up?"

"Trust takes time."

"Marriage makes it mandatory. And legal." Linc took a step forward.

"Easy." Cal's blue eyes were cool. "This isn't about money. Ellie and the baby will never want for anything. We'll make sure of that."

"That baby is mine." Alex wouldn't lose this child, not even to family. Not again. "I'll make sure Ellie and my son or daughter are fine."

"How?" Sam's gaze narrowed.

"By showing up."

"Not good enough." Cal shook his head.

"I agree," Sam said. "Linc is right."

"I frequently am," the brother in question said. "But why do you think so?"

"Marriage." Sam nodded. "It's the only way to be sure. The best protection for our little sister."

Cal nodded. "It's a good plan. Gets my vote, too."

"That's three checks in the yes column," Alex said. "But there's a flaw in your plan."

"None that I can see," Sam said. "Consider it a done deal."

"Tell that to Ellie."

"What are you talking about?" Linc looked at his brothers to see if they understood any better than he did.

Alex could tell they were all in the dark. "Did Ellie tell you I asked her to marry me?"

The men glanced at each other and three blank expressions stared back at him. "No," Sam the spokesman said. "She didn't mention that."

"Then talk to her. I don't expect you'll believe me, but I proposed in Blackwater Lake and again when I saw her yesterday at your parents.'"

"What did she say?" Apparently Linc's hostility balloon had started to leak. His tone had lost the customary animosity.

"If she'd said yes the first time, I wouldn't be here," Alex commented wryly.

"Then you have to bring her around to your way of thinking," Cal said.

The statement reminded Alex of the *Star Trek* series in which the captain would order a subordinate to "make it so" and somehow expect a miracle to happen. Make Ellie marry him? The same woman who'd been determined to climb stairs with a broken ankle? The very one who'd refused to ask for help?

"Have you met your sister?" he asked. "Do you know her? Are you aware that when she makes up her mind, an act of God couldn't change it?"

"Find a way." Sam was obviously used to giving orders that would require a miracle.

"Don't count on it. Her no was pretty emphatic." One by one Alex looked at each of them. "That's all I have to say."

"Alex?" Linc moved forward as he started to turn away. He braced himself. "What?"

"Time will tell whether or not you're a stand-up guy.

But you did the right thing today." There was grudging respect in the other man's eyes.

"Fair enough." Alex held out his hand and Linc took it this time.

He walked back to the elevator and pressed the button for the first level. His shoes clicked on the marble lobby floor as he moved toward the double glass doors.

Bridget looked up from her computer and did a double take. "Looks like it went well."

"How can you tell?"

She pointed. "No more boo-boos on that pretty face."

"Those guys know how to not leave a mark." He waved then left the building.

He almost wished there had been a fight, something to take his mind off the coiled knot in his gut. He'd said what he had to say and got more than expected, which was support for his goal.

Ellie had given him the idea when she'd said the family was on her side. He'd come to see her brothers and change that. Mission accomplished. The Harts no longer had a united front. Three out of five were in his corner, and he was going to need them.

Living with Ellie Hart had shown him how stubborn she was. Oddly enough he missed that. She kept him on his toes and anticipating what came next. She was always a surprise, never boring. But it was more than that. He missed the scent of her skin, her sweet smile first thing in the morning, and the sexy drawl that never failed to make him want her so much it hurt.

He'd come to Dallas for her and would find a way to go to the moon and back if that's what it took to win her. If the time came that he was convinced there was no way to change her mind, he'd have to settle for being close to his child. But he realized after seeing her yesterday that even if he lived next door to her, it wouldn't be close enough to make him happy. He needed more. He needed to fall asleep with her in his arms and wake up with her draped all over him in the morning. To make love with her.

He wanted to live with her and grow old with her. Watch their child grow up and have half a dozen babies with her.

He wouldn't lose his child or Ellie, either.

Alex drove the rental car down the Harts' long, stately driveway and pulled to a stop beneath the portico in front of the imposing estate. There were white columns, balconies, hunter-green shutters framing elegant windows and lots of square footage. A guy didn't have to be in the construction business to know her family was worth a bundle.

They'd have concerns about the guy involved with their daughter, suspicious about his motivation. In his case, money wasn't even on the list. He had more than enough. The simple truth was that he couldn't resist Ellie Hart no matter how hard he tried. And he'd tried pretty damn hard. It was good practice for the perseverance he would need to win her parents over to his cause.

He looked at his watch. Five minutes to zero hour, the time her father had set this meeting after Alex had called.

"Here we go," he muttered, exiting the car.

He moved briskly up the bricked-in walkway to the hunter-green door, a dramatic contrast to the white exterior. It had a gold knocker in the shape of a lion's head. Appropriate, since the lion's den waited for him on the other side of it, he thought. Figuring the thing was only for decorative purposes, he rang the bell.

The housekeeper answered almost immediately. "Mr. McKnight. The Harts are in the family room. I'll show you in."

"That's all right. I remember the way."

The stout, no-nonsense woman shrugged. "Suit yourself."

No need to guess which side the Harts' employee came down on. The professional but cool manner was a big clue.

He walked past the curved stairways, the sound of his shoes echoing off the dark wood floor on the way to the back of the house where Ellie had taken him. She was ignoring his calls, and he was desperate enough to set up a meeting with her parents. He was running out of ideas to get through to her. If this didn't go well, he was prepared to camp out on her doorstep.

From the family room doorway he could see the rear yard, which looked like a park. There was an Olympic-size pool with brick surrounding it. A creek ran through the far side, and he was pretty sure it had an island.

Taking a deep breath, he walked into the room tapping into all the confidence he'd acquired over the years of building his own successful construction company and working with clients as wealthy and powerful as the Harts. They were sitting side by side on the sofa, cups and saucers on the coffee table in front of them. He'd have held out his hand, but neither of them stood up.

"Good afternoon," he said.

Katherine Hart indicated a chair. "Have a seat."

"Thanks."

One didn't refuse an invitation from royalty, and that was what it felt like. They were as impeccably dressed as the last time he'd seen them, and that was impeccable enough for an *InStyle* magazine photo shoot. This wasn't a social call and they didn't offer him refreshments. It set a certain tone and not one likely to work in his favor.

"Thank you both for agreeing to see me."

"We wouldn't have except my son Sam told us what you did yesterday." There was coolness in the man's tone and he had to be feeling something. This was about his only daughter. The ability to control emotion would be a valuable business advantage. No wonder the company was so successful. "It took guts to face my sons."

"Less than you give me credit for. It was the right thing to do."

He felt more like an awkward teenager than when he'd actually been one. This face-to-face meeting with Ellie's parents felt like the most important of his life. Everything was riding on it.

"Still," Katherine said, "The boys can be very intimidating. They're like their father in that way."

After several moments passed, Mr. Hart said, "You asked for this meeting. So what do you want?"

Alex met the man's narrow-eyed gaze and knew exactly what his wife had meant. There was no attempt to put him at ease and every effort to keep him off balance. Their daughter was the first priority and he could respect that.

"First I want to assure you that I'm not after money. McKnight Construction is very successful."

"That's what my investigator said."

"Good." Of course the man would check him out, Alex thought. "I'm here to ask your permission to marry Ellie."

"You don't beat around the bush."

"There's no point, sir. It's why I came."

"According to Sam," the other man said, "you already asked Ellie. Twice. And she turned you down. Even if we gave you our blessing, I don't think it would buy much with her. She doesn't listen to us often. Has a mind of her own, that girl."

"Yes, she does. It's one of the things I like best about her."

Hastings Hart nodded almost imperceptibly. "So you think you know what you'd be getting into."

"I do, sir."

"And you're willing to take her on?"

"Yes, sir." He sat up straight; there was no win in relaxing.

"She's a lot like her mother, so believe it when I say that she's a challenge."

"He's completely serious," his wife said. "I'm not easy, and neither is my daughter."

"I look forward to that."

Anyone worth having was worth working for and Ellie was worth everything. He'd known that as soon as she'd left Blackwater Lake, although it took some time to admit it.

"I'm just not sure we should get involved." The man looked at his wife, who also appeared uncertain.

"Your sons were all in favor of a marriage. It was Linc's idea," he said wryly. "It's what I want, too."

The other man frowned. "So you say."

"Ellie told me her family was on her side, but if I can change your mind, I think that could go a long way toward getting her to accept my proposal."

"At least the baby would have a last name legally, no matter what happens."

Mrs. Hart meant if they divorced. Alex knew from experience how sudden and unexpected change could be, but this time he was less concerned. Ellie was nothing like his ex. Stubborn she was, there was no quit in her, but she was also kind and honest.

"The baby is and always will be mine, too. That's not a legal obligation, but a real privilege." He looked at Ellie's mother. "No matter what happens."

A look of agreement passed between her parents, a couple's communication nurtured and developed over many years of marriage. That's what Alex wanted with their daughter.

Finally Hastings Hart said, "All right. If you can find a way to convince her to say yes, we're on board."

"Thank you, sir."

"Don't thank me yet." The man's eyes turned hard and cold and protective. "If you do anything to hurt my little girl, I promise you'll regret it. Lincoln punching you out will seem like a day at the park and it will be the least of your concerns."

"Understood, sir."

"Really?"

"She told me about the jerk who lied to her. If there's any justice in this world, he and I will cross paths and I'll be the one doing the punching." He looked from one to the other. "I'll never let her down or disappoint her. Most important, I will always tell her the truth."

"Even if she wants to know whether a pair of jeans makes her butt look big?" Her mother's eyes danced with amusement.

"I can't imagine that ever happening." It was the absolute truth. In his opinion, her backside was a work of art.

All humor disappeared when she said, "I'd like to believe what you're saying, but it's difficult. Did she or did she not run away from you?"

"She did, but—"

"No buts." Hastings held up his hand. "She told you no and came home. What's changed?"

"I realized I'm in love with her," he answered simply. "And the first two times I asked, I didn't tell her that."

"Not smart, Mr. McKnight." Mrs. Hart *tsk*ed sympathetically.

"I couldn't agree more. The whole thing was badly

handled, and I'm the first to admit it. I never told her how I feel and it was a big mistake."

"Does that sound familiar, Hasty?"

The older man rolled his eyes. "Are you ever going to let me forget that?"

"Not if I can help it." She smiled fondly at him. "It's a failing of successful men who are accustomed to getting everything without working for it."

"I worked for you, dear."

"And do you regret it?"

"Never." He took her right hand into his own.

"I'm not opposed to working for Ellie," Alex said. "And she's what I want. More than anything, I want a family with her. It's my goal to open a branch of my business here in Dallas so I can be near her and the baby."

"Plan B?"

"Absolutely, sir. It's what a successful man does."

Ellie's father fought a laugh, but couldn't pull it off. "Damn it, son, I like you. The boys were right."

"I'm glad to hear that, Mr. Hart."

"Call me Hastings."

"Would you care for tea or coffee?" His wife asked.

"Thank you, Mrs. Hart. I'd like that very much."

"And I'm Kate." She stood and headed for the doorway.

After his wife left the room, Hastings sat forward, an aggressive posture. "Okay, son, you're going to need a plan to get through to my daughter."

"Do you have something in mind?"

"You bet I do."

"Excellent, sir. I need all the help I can get."

Alex had managed to pull off the practically impossible feat of getting the entire Hart family on his side. These people knew her better than anyone and it would be foolish not to hear them out.

Most important, he wouldn't leave anything to chance. He loved Ellie Hart. and if standing on his head at a Dallas Cowboys football game would convince her to marry him, he'd do it.

He just hoped it wasn't too late.

Chapter Fifteen

"Really, Miss Ellie, you don't need to help me with the dishes."

"I want to, Ina."

Still hiding out with her parents, she'd just finished having dinner with them. Now she was helping with cleanup. She'd gotten used to doing the dishes every night with Alex and missed it—not the dishes so much as him. She'd wade through mud up to her knees and go fishing in the rain if it meant she could spend time with him.

It hurt to think about that. Talk about something else. "How's your family?"

"They're good."

This plump woman with short dark hair and hazel eyes had worked here for at least twenty years. After her husband died suddenly, leaving her with four small children—two girls and two boys—Ellie's parents had given her a job. One of her daughters was a year or two younger than Ellie, and they'd played together as children.

"How's Delaney?"

"Really good. She's getting married."

"That's wonderful." Ellie meant that, even through the sharp stab of envy. "I can't believe you didn't tell me when I first got home."

"The time just didn't seem right." She abruptly turned away and started drying a platter.

"What is it, Ina?"

"Nothing."

"Come on. This is me. I've known you a long time. Y'all are uncomfortable about something. Give it up."

The housekeeper met her gaze. "She's going to have a baby, Miss Ellie."

So, she was uncomfortable about the parallel situation. The only difference was that Delaney was going to marry the father of her baby. "Who's the guy? Do I know him?"

"Your brother Sam introduced them. Peter Scott. He's in banking. Or investments. Something like that."

"Are they in love?" What Ellie really wanted to know was whether or not he was "doing the right thing" or if this was where they'd been headed even if there wasn't a pregnancy.

Ina smiled. "It sure looks that way to me."

"That's wonderful."

"I like Peter very much, but how could I not? He genuinely seems to adore my daughter and makes her happy."

"Then I'm happy for her. And congratulations to you. Y'all are going to be a grandma. Have they set a date yet?"

"I don't know. This just happened."

"If I don't get a wedding invitation, I'll be very unhappy."

Ellie hoped she put just the right balance of sincerity and enthusiasm into her voice. She was happy for her friend and so envious that it must be a sin big enough to send her straight to hell. She wanted to be with Alex, but not out of duty. That would only make him resent her, and she couldn't stand it if he did.

"So, what else is going on?" Ellie asked.

The other woman was putting the dried platter into the cupboard. "Your Mr. McKnight came by yesterday."

"Alex? Here?"

Ina quickly turned to look at her. "Yes. Is there something wrong?"

Good question. "Did he come to see me?"

"Not as far as I know. He called and spoke to your father, and the next thing I knew he was here."

"They talked to him?"

"For a long time. He stayed for dinner."

"What?" She'd gone to Hart Industries to clean up her office, then had dinner with Linc. When she got back to her parents' house they didn't say a word about him being there. Staring at the dinette in the kitchen nook, she asked, "My father, ruthless businessman who gives no quarter, sat at the table and actually ate with Alex?"

"Mrs. Hart requested that they eat in the dining room," Ina confirmed.

The world had gone mad. Her parents, the two people she was counting on to circle the wagons around her, had invited him to dinner?

"What did they talk about?" she asked.

"I was so busy cooking and serving." Again the woman wouldn't look at her.

"Y'all put bits and pieces of information together better than anyone I know. You could be a covert operative for the CIA. Nothing goes on in this house that you don't know about and everyone is aware of that." Ellie put the last plate in the dishwasher then waited for an answer.

"Okay. I heard enough to figure out what happened." She looked proud. "After all, I have a reputation to maintain."

"Tell me."

"This is something you need to talk to your parents about."

"Oh, I intend to. But I'd like to be armed with information before I do."

"Miss Ellie—" There was a maternal expression in the other woman's eyes, a look saying she cared about Ellie as if she were one of her own. "This isn't a business deal or a battle. Miss Kate and Mr. Hastings just want what's best for you. And their first grandchild."

"They have a funny way of showing it by sharing a meal with the man who—"

"Go talk to them about it," Ina suggested. "I'll bring you some tea."

"Thank you." Ellie wished it could be something stronger, but she was pregnant.

She marched into the family room. Two empty dessert plates were on the coffee table. Drinking coffee from china cups, her parents were sitting side by side in the wing chairs. It struck her that they'd done this for years. They were like bookends, holding the family together, presenting a united front.

"How could you?" she said to them.

Kate took a sip from her cup. "What did we do?"

"Threw me under the bus, that's what."

"You heard about Alex being here." Her mother was completely calm, as if she had dinner every night with her daughter's baby daddy.

"Did you think I wouldn't find out? Was it a state secret?"

"Of course not." Hastings put his cup and saucer on the coffee table. "Sit down, Ellie. I have some things to say to you."

"Me first. For starters, what happened to you guys turning Alex away?"

"About that—" Her father crossed one leg over the other, completely relaxed. "It was my plan to do just that until your brothers told me what he did."

"Alex?" It couldn't have been bad, or they wouldn't have fed him dinner. And Linc hadn't said a word to her about anything. "What did he do?"

"He showed up at Hart Industries and faced the boys man to men."

"Unarmed," her mother added.

"Why would he do that?"

"To take responsibility. Declare his intention to be a father. Assure them he hadn't taken advantage of you," her father said.

That was completely true, she thought. One kiss and she'd been his for the taking and there was no doubt in her mind the same thing would happen if he walked in right this minute and took her in his arms. She loved him so much and wouldn't be able to resist him. That was why she'd needed her family to run interference for her.

"So, Sam, Cal and Linc have gone to the dark side, too." It wasn't a question. Obviously her brothers had convinced the folks to see him and hear what he had to say. *Must have been good,* she thought bitterly.

She looked at her father. "I was counting on you to protect me from him, Daddy."

"Look, Ellie, you made it clear that you don't want me hovering. You said it was time to rehabilitate your career and build your reputation without my help. When your mother and I expressed our doubts about you going to Montana, you told us in no uncertain terms that you wanted to stand on your own two feet." Her father leaned forward and met her gaze. "You can't have it both ways."

Darn it all, he had a point, she thought. But since when had he started really listening to her? "That was business, this is personal."

"You don't need protection from him, Ellie. He's a good man."

She knew that better than anyone. He'd taken her in and nursed her when she'd had no one and no place to go. For goodness' sake, he'd washed her hair.

"How did he get to you guys?"

"He said he loves you. And I believe him." Hastings Hart was nothing if not a good judge of character.

"Is love enough?" She hadn't realized she'd said that out loud until her mother answered.

"Love is everything." Kate put her cup down on the table and slid forward on the chair. "Sweetheart, I know you never understood why I gave up my acting career for marriage and motherhood. And I know why you don't get it."

"Good, because I haven't a clue."

"You grew up with three brothers and a father who are high achievers in the business world. You saw them wheel and deal, build things, make money, and all of that is revered and praised in the Hart family. You just want us to be proud of you."

Ellie nodded, her mouth trembling. She sat down on the love seat closest to her mother's chair. When she could speak, she said, "It's really important to me."

"We are proud of you and we love you very much." Kate

reached over and took her hand. "The only achievement we want is for you to be happy. That makes us proudest of all."

"It's not enough."

"That's where you're wrong. I made the decision I did because I was deeply and completely in love with your father. And I am still head over heels about him to this day. I never had a single regret. It never occurred to me that I gave up anything when Hastings Hart asked for my hand. He's all I ever wanted."

"Really?"

"Truly." She smiled when her husband leaned over and kissed her cheek. "Ellie, if you want a career, there are ways to make it work, but you need to start with a good supportive man. A man like Alex."

"He asked me to marry him, but never said a word about his feelings. He's just trying to do the right thing." She was so used to living in the bad place it was dangerous to let herself believe in anything good. If she did that, she'd have to admit that she blew her chance to be happy. So much for making her family proud. "I won't settle for less than love."

"He's trying to do the right thing because he does love you. A person would have to be completely clueless not to see it," her mother said. "The thing is, sweetie, men like Alex McKnight don't come along every day. Maybe once in a lifetime if you're very, very lucky."

"I don't know," she said. "Before the baby we agreed that this wouldn't be serious. I have no reason to think he's changed his mind about that."

"He came after you," her mother pointed out. "He did the manly thing facing your father and brothers. That speaks well of his intentions."

"You need to talk to him," her father said.

"I have, and it didn't change anything."

"Telling him you're pregnant then coming home to your father and me is not talking."

Pride wanted to say that communicating with him was a really bad plan, but it was time to stop being stupid. Eventually she would have to see him, anyway. "Do you know where he's staying here in Dallas?"

"Dallas? You didn't know?" Her mother looked surprised.

"What?"

"He's gone back to Blackwater Lake. He said you seemed very sure that you didn't want to marry him."

"So he left town," Ellie said. "Seems to me he gave up pretty quick for a man in love."

Her father glanced at his wife. "I promised your mother I'd never bring this up again, but it has to be said. When that lying, adulterous jerk cost you your first job, you walked away without a fight, without telling anyone at work what he did to you."

"No one would have believed me."

"Your family did and no one else matters," her father pointed out. "The bottom line is whether or not you win, you've got to fight back if you want something bad enough. At least you'll never have to look back and regret letting something get away."

Her mother nodded. "As is often the case, Hasty, you're completely right about that. Ellie, that horrible experience cost you a job. You're beautiful, bright and talented with a fabulously successful career ahead of you. But if you don't confront Alex and let him know how you feel, it will cost you happiness."

And her family's respect. It was hard to argue when they were right.

"Y'all are the smartest parents in the world." She stood,

then leaned down to kiss first her mother, then her father. "I know what I have to do."

Hastings Hart smiled proudly at his daughter. "That's my little girl."

Ellie drove up Main Street in Blackwater Lake and took everything in as if she hadn't seen it for years instead of days. The town, mountains and lake touched a place inside her where she'd never been touched before. She cared deeply about cautious expansion and meticulous preservation of land and natural resources.

Mostly, though, she desperately cared about Alex and couldn't wait to see him.

She stopped at the red light and glanced over at the Grizzly Bear Diner, the Tanya's Treasures gift shop and the dry cleaner on the corner. There was comfort, charm and warmth here. It was why Alex had come back from California with the woman carrying the child he'd thought was his. And he was willing to give up this beautiful place to be near their child.

The truth was that Alex McKnight had touched her soul. He might not feel the same way, but if she didn't find out one way or the other, she'd never be able to hold her head high in the future.

The only time you failed was when you failed to try.

The light turned green, and she continued on until Mercy Medical Clinic came into view. After turning into the parking lot she stopped the rental car next to Alex's truck. It was déjà vu—the long drive from the airport that had ended right in this same spot. Full circle, but everything had changed, and not just the fact that the expansion project had risen from foundation to finished.

When she'd first arrived her goal had been about a job to build a résumé, but now she had to find her life.

First she wanted to inspect the clinic addition. There was a banner on the side announcing the date of the grand opening, which was about four weeks away. Through a rear door added during construction, she walked inside, where carpenters installed cabinets and painters were rolling a soothing shade of light gold on the walls. Following the hall, she entered the existing waiting area and saw the receptionist counter and window. It was lunchtime so no patients were there.

The room was empty except for Martha Spooner, who was talking to nurse Ginny Irwin. They looked over but didn't seem all that surprised to see her. Maybe the two women knew something she didn't.

"Hi, Ellie."

"Nice to see you, Martha. Are you all right?"

"Yes. Why?"

"This is a medical clinic, Spooner." The nurse grinned. "The fact is, Ellie, she's not here to see the doc. We've been friends for a long time. She came to pick me up for lunch."

"That's a relief. I'm glad y'all are well."

"Never better." The older woman slid her hands into the pockets of her jeans and looked her over. "How are you?"

"How's the ankle?" Ginny asked.

Ellie glanced down at her high-top sneakers and realized that was another change. "It feels pretty good. And the hardware in it didn't set off metal detectors at the airport."

"Ben will be glad to hear that."

"He will," Martha agreed, giving her friend a look that said, *Don't change the subject.* "But I was asking how you're *feeling.*"

Emphasis on the last word told Ellie that she meant the baby, but also gave her wiggle room in case she didn't want to talk about that in front of anyone else. There was no point in pretending; eventually the whole town would know she and Alex were having a baby. This was about taking charge. No more running away.

"I'm still having some morning sickness, but my obstetrician says it should get better in a few weeks."

Now Ginny looked surprised and gave Martha a you-held-out-on-me look. "Congratulations."

"Thanks." She smiled and added, "I'm very excited. Surprised, but happy. So is Alex."

"You know," Ginny said, "Jill and Adam were disappointed when you left. They wanted you to draw up plans to build their house."

"And you owe me a kitchen," Martha reminded her.

"I'll give Jill a call." She looked at Alex's housekeeper. "And I'm ready to start when you are."

"Good enough." The woman nodded her approval. "It's about time that man hooked up with a woman who's coming back instead of leaving."

Ellie didn't know about the hooking-up part, but she was here. It was up to Alex whether or not she stayed.

Martha was looking past her, eyes narrowed. "Hi, Alex. Look who came back."

Ellie's heart pounded as she turned. He was a sight for sore eyes and an even sorer heart. He looked tired, but otherwise he was his same solid, sexy self in jeans, T-shirt and boots.

"Hi," she said. "I was planning to stop in the construction trailer after looking things over here."

"I saw you pull in," he said.

Had he been anxious to see her or just didn't believe she was going to see him? Hopefully the first one, she thought.

"Ginny, we need to go to lunch. Now," Martha prodded.

"Right behind you, Spooner."

Ellie never took her eyes from Alex's, but somehow

knew when the women were gone and they were completely alone. "How are you?"

"Okay. You?"

She knew he meant the baby. "Everything's perfect."

He looked her over and when he got to her feet, the corner of his mouth turned up. "Pink high-tops. Is that a Texas look?"

"Not really. More Montana practical."

"The short skirt makes a statement."

Good or bad? But she didn't ask. "I packed in a hurry."

"Why are you here, Ellie?" His eyes darkened. "Why did you come back?"

"I'm here to finish what we started." One way or the other.

"You're not talking about the clinic."

It wasn't a question, but she shook her head. "My family may have mentioned that I'd be stupid to not express to you my feelings. Although he could do with a little less stubborn pride where I'm concerned, my daddy doesn't tolerate stupidity in a Hart."

Alex moved closer, near enough to pull her into his arms. But he didn't touch her. "I'm listening."

She'd rehearsed this speech on the long, lonely drive from the airport. "First of all, I want to apologize for not sticking to the rules of the fling."

"We both agreed not to get emotionally involved," he said.

"Right. I didn't plan to fall in love with you, Alex. It just happened." She took a deep breath because this was the part where she bared her soul. "I understand if you don't want me—"

"Oh, God, Ellie—" In a heartbeat he'd folded her against his chest. "I want you more than anything in the world."

He cupped her cheek in his palm, then lowered his mouth to hers while she slid her arms around his waist. As communication went, this said everything. His mouth was greedy and he held her as if he'd never let her go. His heart pounded against hers and the two beat as one.

Both of them were breathless when he pulled back and looked into her eyes. "I've asked you this question twice, but neglected to say the single most important part."

"Okay. Try again."

"Third time's the charm." His eyes turned dark and intensity vibrated through him. "Ellie Hart, I want you to marry me as soon as possible, and it has nothing to do with duty or obligation because of the baby. The truth is I'm in love with you and I have been from the moment you refused to have a drink with me after work."

"No way," she said.

"Way." Still cupping her cheek, he brushed his thumb over her lips. "The thing is, I've jumped in with both feet before, and this was so fast, so unexpected."

"Like lightning?"

"Exactly. No man wants to get zapped like that."

"No woman, either," she said.

"It was the last thing I wanted and was too proud and stubborn to admit the truth. But it's why I brought you home with me when you broke your ankle. It scared me how much I wanted to take care of you, protect you. So the best strategy I could come up with was a fling."

"I see." That was a lie, but she was beginning to believe there would be plenty of time to sort things out. She loved where this was going.

"The reality is that I couldn't resist you. I love you, Ellie Hart."

"Then why did y'all leave Dallas?"

"That was your father's suggestion. He thought it would

be a good plan, a way to get you to see reason. Your mom agreed. Something about letting a bird go to see if it comes back and is really yours."

Again, she was too happy to question how convoluted that strategy was. Although it had worked, and she got here as quick as she could. "I knew my parents were on your side."

"In a good way. Your brothers like me, too."

She smiled. "Does that mean you wouldn't mind living in Dallas?"

The truth was in his eyes when he said, "If you'll be my wife, I'd live on the moon. As long as we're together, anywhere you are makes me happy."

"Okay, then. Nothing would make me happier than to be your wife and stay here in Blackwater Lake."

His grin was so unexpected, so filled with joy, that it nearly brought her to her knees. He lifted her and swung her around. "Anything for you."

She laughed and held on, because life with this man was going to be quite a ride. When he set her back on her feet she said, "Deny it all you want, but I know the truth."

"Which is?"

"You always have been and always will be my Mc-Knight in shining armor."

* * * * *

COMING NEXT MONTH
from Harlequin® Special Edition®
AVAILABLE JULY 23, 2013

#2275 THE MAVERICK'S SUMMER LOVE
Montana Mavericks: Rust Creek Cowboys
Christyne Butier
Handsome carpenter Dean Pritchett comes to Rust Creek Falls, Montana, to help repair flood damage. But can single mom Shelby, who has a checkered past, fix Dean's wounded heart?

#2276 IT'S A BOY!
The Camdens of Colorado
Victoria Pade
Widow Heddy Hanrahan is about to give up her bakery when struggling single dad Lang Camden comes to her rescue. Can Heddy overcome her past to find love with her knight in a shining apron?

#2277 WANTED: A REAL FAMILY
The Mommy Club
Karen Rose Smith
When physical therapist Sara Stevens's home burns down, her ex-patient Jase invites Sara and her daughter to live near him. But when sparks of a personal nature ignite, Sara wonders if she's made a mistake....

#2278 HIS LONG-LOST FAMILY
Those Engaging Garretts!
Brenda Harlen
When Kelly Cooper returned to Pinehurst, New York, she wanted her daughter, Ava, to know her father—not to rekindle a romance with Jackson Garrett. But sometimes first love deserves a second chance....

#2279 HALEY'S MOUNTAIN MAN
The Colorado Fosters
Tracy Madison
Outsider Gavin Daugherty isn't looking for companionship, so he's taken aback when Steamboat Springs, Colorado, sweetheart Haley Foster befriends him. When their friendship blossoms into something more, will Gavin run for the hills?

#2280 DATE WITH DESTINY
Helen Lacey
Grace Preston moved away from Crystal Point, Australia, after school, leaving her family—and heartbroken boyfriend, Cameron—behind. When a troubled Grace returns home, she finds that some loves just can't remain in the past....

You can find more information on upcoming Harlequin® titles, free excerpts and more at www.Harlequin.com.

HSECNM0713

REQUEST YOUR FREE BOOKS!
2 FREE NOVELS PLUS 2 FREE GIFTS!

⊞ HARLEQUIN®

SPECIAL EDITION
Life, Love & Family

HSEI3R

SPECIAL EXCERPT FROM

H HARLEQUIN®

SPECIAL EDITION

*Handsome carpenter Dean Pritchett comes to
Rust Creek Falls to help rebuild the town after the
Great Montana Flood and meets a younger woman with a
checkered past. Can Shelby Jenkins repair the damage to
this cowboy's heart?*

***

Shelby laid a hand on his arm. "Please, don't stop. I like listening to you."

"Yeah?"

She nodded, trying to erase the tingling sensation that danced from her palm to her elbow thanks to the warmth of his skin.

"My brothers and I have worked on projects together, but usually it's just me and whatever piece of furniture I'm working on."

"Solitary sounds good to me. My job is nothing but working with people. Sometimes that can be hard, too."

"Especially when those people aren't so nice?"

Shelby nodded, wrapping her arms around her bent knees as she stared out at the nearby creek.

Dean leaned closer, brushing back the hair that had fallen against her cheek, his thumb staying behind to move back and forth across her cheek.

Her breath caught, then vanished completely the moment he touched her. She was frozen in place, her arms locked around her knees, held captive by the simple press of his thumb.

He gently lifted her head while lowering his. The warmth of

his breath floated across her skin, his green eyes darkening to a deep jade as he looked down at her.

Before their lips could meet, Shelby broke free.

Dropping her chin, she kept her gaze focused on the sliver of blanket between them as heat blazed across her cheeks.

Dean stilled for a moment, then eased away. "Okay. This is a bit awkward."

"I'm sorry." She closed her eyes, not wanting to see the disappointment, or worse, in his eyes as the apology rushed past her lips. "I haven't— It's been a long time since I've—"

"It's okay, Shelby. No worries. I'll wait."

She looked up and found nothing in his gaze but tenderness mixed with banked desire. "You will? Why?"

"Because when the time is right, kissing you is going to be so worth it."

***

We hope you enjoyed this sneak peek at
USA TODAY *bestselling author Christyne Butler's*
new Harlequin® Special Edition® book,
THE MAVERICK'S SUMMER LOVE,
the next installment in
MONTANA MAVERICKS:
RUST CREEK COWBOYS,
a brand-new six-book continuity
launching in July 2013!

SADDLE UP AND READ 'EM!

Looking for another great Western read? Check out these August reads from the HOME & FAMILY category!

THE LONG, HOT TEXAS SUMMER by Cathy Gillen Thacker
McCabe Homecoming
Harlequin American Romance

HOME TO THE COWBOY by Amanda Renee
Harlequin American Romance

HIS FOREVER VALENTINE by Marie Ferrarella
Forever, Texas
Harlequin American Romance

THE MAVERICK'S SUMMER LOVE by Christyne Butler
Montana Mavericks
Harlequin Special Edition

Look for these great Western reads AND MORE available wherever books are sold or visit
www.Harlequin.com/Westerns